LaserWriter II

LASERWRITER II

TAMARA SHOPSIN

MCD
Farrar, Straus and Giroux
New York

MCD
Farrar, Straus and Giroux
120 Broadway, New York 10271

Library of Congress Cataloging-in-Publication Data
Names: Shopsin, Tamara, author.
Title: LaserWriter II : a novel / Tamara Shopsin.
Description: First edition. | New York : MCD / Farrar, Straus and
    Giroux, 2021.
Identifiers: LCCN 2021019905 | ISBN 9780374602574 (hardcover)
Subjects: LCSH: Computer technicians—Fiction | Apple computer—
    Fiction. | Computer printers—Fiction. | GSAFD: Bildungsromans.
Classification: LCC PS3619.H659 L37 2021 | DDC 813/.6—dc23
LC record available at https://lccn.loc.gov/2021019905

Designed by Tamara Shopsin

Our books may be purchased in bulk for promotional, educational,
or business use. Please contact your local bookseller or the Macmillan Corporate
and Premium Sales Department at 1-800-221-7945, extension 5442,
or by email at MacmillanSpecialMarkets@macmillan.com.

www.mcdbooks.com • www.fsgbooks.com
Follow us on Twitter, Facebook, and Instagram at @mcdbooks

1   3   5   7   9   10   8   6   4   2

for

LaserWriter II

The elevator is crowded. Not with people. With an
eighteen-inch monitor, two keyboards, a bulbous shape
swaddled in a garbage bag, and a curvy black laptop.
The laptop is tucked under the chin of a man with tears
in his eyes.

Bong. Everyone gets out of the elevator, though the
building has eight more floors till the roof. Photos
of Albert Einstein, Picasso, and Gandhi are tacked to
the walls. Down the hall, a door is propped open by a
defunct dot matrix printer.

Inside the fourth floor, a red lever is pushed for a green
ticket. There are no walls, the space is full—full of
people and machines, old and new. Wooden theater
seats snap open and shut. A redheaded woman sways on
a porch swing, drinking cold Coca-Cola from a bottle.
Next to her on the swing, in the sweetheart seat, is a
Quadra 700 tower.

"19" is shouted, and the number flicks to life, displayed
in black and white on a modified Mac Plus computer
mounted near the ceiling. Below the Mac a girl wears
red sneakers and holds no computer. 19 is Claire's age,
not her ticket. Her ticket says "29," but she doesn't

3

need it. She folds the ticket until she can fold it no more and puts it deep in one of her many pockets.

Next to her people read magazines and newspapers, they stare at the pressed tin ceilings and wood floors, at plastic dinosaurs arranged in the dirt of a ficus, at the Mac Plus, waiting for its number to advance, they stare everywhere but at each other. This is after all New York City.

Glances are stolen.

Especially at the woman eating a sack of hulled sunflower seeds one at a time, and David Bowie in the corner listening to a Discman.

Claire worries: They will call 29, and no one will answer. When they advance to number 30 she will be told she screwed up by taking the green ticket. "NO JOB FOR YOU." will scroll across the Mac Plus, and a sad Mac with "x"s for eyes will flash on and off, making a death chime.

"20" is called. The redhead and her Quadra 700 waddle up to the section of the room marked "Intake."

An employee with purple hair yells out "29," and Claire looks up.

Apple was founded on ripping off phone companies. Steve Jobs and Woz built the personal computer, but first they built pocket-size blue boxes—blue boxes that tricked telecom computers into placing calls to Italy and beyond.

The early days of Apple were filled with Nerf balls, remote control cars, and pirate flags. Susan Kare, the designer of the sad Mac icon, made portraits that were 32 pixels wide for fun. The plastic case of the first Macintosh computer was cast with the signatures of its developers, because it was a work of art. Claire's family had this first Mac, and an Apple IIc before it, and then whatever computer Apple made next, forever.

Claire remembers the fragile floppy disks that held her favorite games. One let her construct pinball machines that could then be played. She would drag all the flippers and bumpers onto a rectangle, trying to make the white dot ricochet forever. She learned what typhoid, cholera, and dysentery were from playing *The Oregon Trail*, a game built of manifest destiny and paragraphs of green text. In MacPaint, Claire used the selection tool to draw squares over and over, mesmerized by the marching ants of the marquee.

No death chime sounds.

The employee with purple hair advances the number on the Mac Plus and calls out "30." A woman whose favorite color must be black stands up with ticket 30 and a laptop in her tattooed hands.

Claire stands, too. She walks toward the door. A woman in an apron decorated with a giant question mark sits on a stool keeping watch over the waiting room. Claire approaches her but is beat to it by a man. He asks Question Mark about picking up his repaired computer. Claire recognizes the man, but she doesn't know from where. He is skinny with bulging eyes and a sort of painful voice. Question Mark points the man to a counter beside her.

Claire didn't notice the counter before, despite a hanging sign that says "PICK UPS," and a large arrow that bounces on a spring.

Familar man frees up Question Mark and begins to talk with the worker behind the Pick Up counter.

"He is a plumber . . . or an actor?" Question Mark says in a soft whisper to Claire, who thinks the same thing but doesn't say it out loud.

"Are you ticket 29?" Question Mark asks.
Claire takes a moment. "Um. I'm here for a job interview. The listing was on a Mac message board?"
"Ahh, okay, you need to see David."

There is a commotion at the Pick Up counter. Claire and Question Mark look over.

"You just said 'Hey aren't you an actor, aren't you Steve Buscemi?'" familiar man says, his painful voice agitated. "Yes, but to pick up a machine you need ID. It is the rule. I need to write the number down. You could be pretending to be Steve Buscemi to get his computer, which aside from being valuable has personal information," the man working the Pick Up desk explains.
"Can you make an exception? I am clearly Steve Buscemi."
"Hang on."

The Pick Up desk worker slides over to Question Mark and they huddle in place.

"Can I skip the ID part?" Pick Up worker asks.
"Maybe you should ask David," Question Mark says.
"No, I'm scared of David. Could you just come over and make sure it really is Steve Buscemi? And we'll put it in the notes and then both initial it?"
"You mean so we both can get in trouble?"
"Customer is wait-ting," Pick Up worker says, tilting his head toward Steve Buscemi.
Question Mark turns to Claire. "I'll be right back, can you make sure everyone who enters takes a ticket?"

Claire nods.

"Hang on, you need a ticket," Claire says, and points to the ticket machine.

"Do you know how long the wait will be?" a woman asks, taking a ticket.
"No. Sorry."
"Don't you work here?"
"No, not really."

Question Mark returns. She launches into a small speech on the fluid nature of identity and the soul. The speech concludes with the fact that David's office is near the bathroom.

Shelves of vintage radios and telephones make up the bounds of the office. A man whose suspenders curve around his belly introduces himself as David. Claire shakes his hand and notices he has no shoes on. They sit down at his old oak desk, in old oak chairs that swivel.

A wire runs above David's desk. Claire stares at the floating line that has a set of clips and some kind of motor attached. David sees her staring and grabs a baby-blue Sony microfloppy disk from a drawer. He clips the disk to the wire and gives it a little tug. The motor starts and the disk begins to float leftward toward another oak desk. "That's Dick's desk," David explains as he tugs at the wire again, making the disk float back to them.

"So why do you want to work at Tekserve?" David asks, putting the microfloppy back in his drawer.

"I love Macs," Claire says before the drawer can close.

David asks if she has any technical training or mechanical ability.

She has no training but is pretty sure she is mechanical. Claire mentions drilling a hole into her desk to hold a pencil, and that she repaired her father's gray plastic suitcase with epoxy.

"Have you ever used FileMaker?" David asks.
"No, I don't even know what it is," Claire answers.

The interview is over.

TIME

OUT

Louis J. Schweitzer was rich: the best kind of rich. He bought his wife gondolas, theaters, and a taxi medallion. He gifted his barber with a shop in exchange for the promise of haircuts any time of day for life. When Louis' favorite radio station played too many ads, he bought it and replaced the ads with poetry.

The radio station was WBAI, and a few years after buying it, in 1960, Louis gave the station to the Pacifica Foundation, a nonprofit radio network located in Berkeley, California. Listener sponsored with no ads, Pacifica could do whatever it wanted, which was to fight McCarthy and broadcast the Beat poets, in full.

Pacifica took over WBAI and turned it from a classical station to a counterculture hub with a mishmash of programming. Every weeknight from 12:00 a.m. to 6:00 a.m. WBAI aired a show called Radio Unnameable, hosted by Bob Fass. It was a new kind of radio. Yes, music was played, but sometimes backward, or two records at the same time. There were long calls from listeners, with political rants encouraged. The show was unscripted and flowed from Bob Fass's lips in a steady stream. Unnameable was beloved by night-shift workers, anarchists, musicians, and David.

In ninth grade, David began volunteering on Unnameable. He was a technical kid and felt at home in the studio, with its knobs and switches.

David edited tape loops, like Bob Fass saying, "less is sometimes more" over and over. He made recordings of the show, but mostly he hung out. When Fass learned that David was doing speed, he scolded him and told him not to take that awful drug, acid was much better. Soon David was volunteering at the station on weekends, too, making field recordings of events like Earth Day, answering the phones for pledge drives, and harboring a crush on the neopagan journalist Margot Adler.

After turning on and tuning in, David dropped out. He was kicked out of his prep school for underachieving. It was 1970, and he was 17 years old. He went to work at WBAI full-time as a radio engineer, riding his bike to 30 East 39th Street from his parents' apartment on 78th and West End.

WBAI was to move into an old church on East 62nd Street, though first the church had to be built out with studios and circuits. David helped do this, and so did Dick, a new employee. Dick was older and raised in Queens. He had graduated from college and landed a dream job as an engineer at RCA. But RCA was working with the military, and Dick wore bell-bottoms. So he dropped out, crossed the country and back, listening to antiwar radio nonstop.

Drinking Coca-Cola was David's religion. An old Coke machine came with the church. It dispensed cans. David, being devout, converted the machine to bottles.

The nave was split into control rooms and filled with equipment. Soon the church was up and running. Dick was hired as a full-time employee. He and David continued to work together along with another technician named Mike.

When Mike's car backed up, it would warn pedestrians with a "ding dong ding dong." He had wired a doorbell to the reverse of his car engine.

Mike was a self-taught genius.

This was partly because he had dropped out of high school.

He helped friends wire their electric meters to run backward, he hooked his telephone up to his stereo so he could dial a song, and he built sound consoles that were mythic in the music industry.

Across the country, in a kitchen in San Jose, California, Margaret Wozniak thought her son might like an article that she read in *Esquire* magazine. It was fall of 1971, and the article was "Secrets of the Little Blue Box" by Ron Rosenbaum.

At the time, all telephones had dial tones, and most were the size of an adult shoe. A band of misfits known as "phreaks" figured out you could trick the phone company into placing free calls. The phreaks discovered that the entire telephone system was controlled by a combination of six master tones.

2600 hz was the key frequency. It was the sound used to switch into the system. The tone made the phone company think the call had hung up, but it hadn't. It was as if the phreak hid behind a dinosaur, avoiding the flashlight's beam, getting to spend all night in the museum.

This 2600 hz tone was first made by a blind boy with perfect pitch named Joe who whistled it into his receiver. When kind volunteers came to read aloud to the boy, he requested technical telephone manuals rather than adventure novels like *Treasure Island*.

Soon a plastic whistle that came as a prize in a box of Cap'n Crunch cereal was discovered to blow at exactly 2600 hz. Electronic organs were used, recorded to a cassette and played back at a higher speed. Phreaking started to spread. "Blue boxes" were created—an electronic device loaded with all the tones needed, at the push of a button.

Halfway through the article that his mom recommended, Steve Wozniak (Woz), a freshman in college, could hardly contain himself. He called his 17-year-old friend Steve Jobs and read the rest of the story aloud.

The first blue box Woz and Jobs built almost worked. But the box was analog made, with resistors and capacitors that were imprecise, their frequency fluctuating with hot and cold.

Woz decided to design a digital blue box that would be more reliable. It was a sweep of brilliance that used computer chips, a quartz crystal, and minimal power consumption.

One of the first free calls Woz and Jobs made was to the Pope. Jobs thought they could sell the blue boxes for $150 a pop, and he was right.

Woz has said that his blue box circuit was the most elegant he ever designed, more beautiful than even the ones he later made for the Apple I and II.

Claire had eight siblings. She was the middle child. Unless you counted the twins as one birth, like her mother did.

But sharing the Apple II was easy—half the tribe wasn't interested in the box and the other half understood how special it was. And with that special understanding came the absolute knowledge that it was a human right to be shared equally.

The first phone call Claire received was when she was 10 years old.

Claire was sitting on the floor making an ugly pot holder on a loom. She wore a black hat with a brim that touched halfway down her spine and became her shoulders.

The phone mounted on the wall rang, and her little sister answered. Its pink coiled cord swayed in her sister's hands, but it turned out to be a call for their older sister. Her older sister got on and found that the caller was looking for their brother, who after some time came to the phone and was asked for his younger brother, and this went on and on until the person on the other end of the phone asked for Claire.

And everyone immediately realized it was a prank call.

"Maybe tell them I am dead," Claire said.

"Oh I see you want to speak to Claire? She died last week—you just missed her," her brother said and hung up.

It used to be there was one phone company, "Ma Bell," and she made sure every single telephone call cost money to make. Even a prank call.

Unlimited calling plans didn't exist, save if you had a blue box or the ability to whistle in perfect pitch. Every time you dialed a phone there was a charge, unless the person on the other end was someone like David. Unbeknownst to his mom, David had installed a black box on their line. With a black box it still cost money to make outgoing calls, but every call the phone received was 100% free for the person calling. Bob Fass had one, too.

This was a goodwill thing, the person calling might not even know. The black box should have been orange because it was pretty much the opposite of a blue box.

When the Vietnam War ended, WBAI lost its pull. There was a pivot toward salsa music and a staff revolt. Dick, David, and Mike left the station and started a company together called Current Designs.

In the beginning they ran the company from Dick's loft on West 23rd Street. It was a floor-through with plants pressed against the windows and Persian cats curled atop vintage radios. Rather than a couch, Dick had an old porch swing bolted to the ceiling.

Current Designs' big client was Acoustiguide. Acoustiguide provided audio tours for museums across the world using specially designed tape players. These tape players were manufactured at Dick's dining room table.

At first, they just altered existing tape players, making the mechanisms quieter and the machines more sturdy. A Bulgarian named Lyuben was hired to help the three with soldering. Then another employee was added, and another, until they were renting the floor below and building the tape players from scratch.

It was the early eighties. Personal computers had just been born but were thick in the air. Dick, David, and Mike went to every computer store in New York they could. This wasn't hard, there were only a few stores in existence. IBM, Commodore, Sinclair, Zenith—none of the computers were right. Then in January of 1984 at Macy's department store on a white pedestal they found their Goldilocks Planet.

The Macintosh was marketed by Apple as "insanely great." The beige box had no hard drive—its system software lived on a floppy disk and ran only two programs. It was insane. Dick, David, and Mike each bought one on the spot.

All the other personal computers used a command line. They wouldn't do anything until you typed a command. When the machines booted up, a cursor blinked blankly at you. When the Macintosh booted up, a miniature Macintosh smiled at you.

Current Designs started drawing their circuit diagrams in MacPaint and sending them to Japan to be manufactured. The drawings wowed the Japanese, who sent back perfect components. The Macintosh went from 128k to 512k. A LaserWriter printer was added, software accelerators were installed. Soon the machines became involved in all of Current Designs' projects.

Acoustiguide wasn't Current Designs' only client. Current Designs designed and manufactured pillboxes with alarms, radios that played advertisements on demand, and listening stations that could withstand the grubby hands of New Yorkers. But Acoustiguide was the steady client. The other work ebbed and flowed. Current Designs now had thirty employees, though it still felt like a clubhouse with its own ten-cent Coke machine.

A contract was signed by Acoustiguide with a factory in China to manufacture their tape players at half the price.

The steady work ebbed.

Current Designs started to shrink till it was back in Dick's loft. The Coke machine was put in his kitchen.

Steve Jobs was proud of how quiet the Macintosh was. Other PCs whirred and whined, but not the Macintosh. This was because it had no fan.

David's Macintosh failed first. The repair shop he called knew what the problem was without even looking at it. As Macs aged, they would all overheat. With no fan to cool the machine, the power supply would burn out. Only two shops in New York could do the repair. Both said it would cost $350.

Dick, David, and Mike repaired and built audio equipment for a living, why couldn't they fix a computer? They could. They did. Soon they were replacing power supplies for friends at $135 per.

Word got out about the $135 power repair, and they began doing the fix for friends of friends. With Acoustiguide out, Lyuben switched from soldering tape players all day to soldering Macintosh power supplies. People would drop their dead computers in Dick's living room, and pick them up a week later with a one-year warranty.

Apple gave only a ninety-day warranty, and it took them two or three weeks. Mac Emporium on Madison Avenue hired Current Designs to fix Macintoshes wholesale.

Current Designs had steady work again, and it started
to grow. A musician was hired full-time for his
Macintosh enthusiasm, not his audio background.

Dick and David loved fixing Macs. Mike not so much.
It was unanimous—Mike would run Current Designs
on his own, taking all the audio repair and design
work. Dick and David would keep the Macintosh work
and start a new company called Tekserve.

TIME

IN

Claire is hired on the spot.

The job has perks:
1. Macs at cost.
2. Free lunch on Wednesdays.
   Free breakfast Thursdays.
3. Full health care that starts right away. "None of this trial crap," as David put it.

Claire will be working intake. Intake = triage, but the patients are computers, not humans. Patty, the employee with purple hair, is excited to train Claire in the Tao of intake.

Away from David, Patty confides to Claire that this is her first time training someone, but she will do her best not to mess up Claire's future self.

Patty is 23, with a similar past to Claire except her favorite floppy disk constructed buildings, not pinball machines. The game was Hard Hat Mack. As a little girl, Patty loved to lay I-beams and collect lunch boxes while avoiding 8-bit OSHA safety inspectors.

They pass a terrarium. Patty points out a lizard to Claire. It is hidden beneath what looks like a bunch of fresh dill on steroids. "That's Newton. If you have a hard intake—and you will—my advice is to come here and just watch him for a little."

"What do you mean by hard?" Claire asks.

But Patty is gone, lost in the terrarium, watching Newton's little feet shift over neon decorative gravel toward a tilted circuit board that he shimmies up and mounts. Newton sits still as stone, matched only by Patty's steady gaze.

Claire coughs on purpose. Patty looks at her. "What do you mean by hard?" Claire asks.

"It can be brutal. A customer will react to a bad diagnosis like they were told their mother has cancer. Watching someone crumble like that is hard. And then on the other side of the coin, some customers are just total jerkwads."

Patty leads Claire past an invisible line. No chain, wall, or sign blocks the back of Tekserve, but it is clear they have crossed a border. Patty points out the staff kitchen with a big table and an office that belongs to "Thor & Monica."

Then Patty introduces Monica, who is all smiles with wide eyes and a ponytail.

Monica was born in Germany, but grew up in New Jersey. She built a computer with her dad when she was 8, which was the only way you could have a home computer at the time. She learned to program in Pascal and Basic for fun. In her sophomore year of college, Monica interned at the independent record label Beggars Banquet. She was paid in CDs that she would sell to Kim's records on St. Marks Place for cash—very little cash.

A bum always sat outside Kim's with a fishing pole. He was a teenage runaway, though he was no longer teenage.

The bum's name was Picasso. He had a shaved head and wore a leather jacket that was like a preschooler's toy with buckles, snaps, and chains. It would jingle as he climbed on top of a telephone booth or any perch he could find, his cup set on the street below. All day he would sit and fish, a dollar baited on the hook, though it was mostly coins he caught in his cup.

Picasso lived in a squat on Avenue B called Big Squat. Claire knew this squat well. On Sundays when she was younger, she would volunteer for a chapter of Food Not

Bombs that operated out of Big Squat's kitchen. Food Not Bombs collected food waste from restaurants and groceries. That food was then boiled in a mammoth pot with lentils and way too much cumin for far too long. The pot would be loaded into a shopping cart and wheeled to Tompkins Square Park, where it was emptied by anyone who needed to eat.

Food Not Bombs and Big Squat were collectively run, nonhierarchical, antiauthoritarian, grassroots, and all that.

Both collectives seemed to function well. Big Squat's crazy quilt of a kitchen was clean—at least taking into consideration the communal aspect of it. Food Not Bombs had self-created and self-regulated chapters all over the world that fed thousands of people.

Claire was drawn to the ideals of these collectives, a.k.a. anarchism. Not the anarchism in Sex Pistols songs that talked about Antichrist and wanting to destroy, not knowing what they want but knowing how to get it—that kind of bullshit. Claire was drawn to the type of anarchy that believed in small communities and held the promise of a just society. Everyone had said, "life is not fair," but maybe it could be.

Big Squat was also used for concerts. They had a makeshift stage in the basement. The music was hardcore, punk, sometimes ska or crust, but mostly a band named Hookworm68. This was because all the members of Hookworm68 lived in Big Squat.

The band had begun as "Hookworm," but they found out there was already a band named that in Dayton, Ohio. After a two-second meeting the New York Hookworm added "68" to their name, the way one does to a password to make it stronger.

The "68" was to suggest the French Situationists, not the sex act minus 1.

Hookworm68's lead singer was named Herpes. Herpes was obsessed with Guy Debord and the student uprising of May '68. Half of Hookworm68's songs were based on French graffiti slogans, and the other half were not very good.

Everyone had a crush on Herpes—girls, boys, men, women, and in-between. This was despite the fact that he was named Herpes and, to put it in the kindest words, self-destructive.

Claire had the mildest infatuation possible with
Herpes. It manifested itself in two ways. 1: She went
to every concert Hookworm68 played. This meant
one concert a week and a lot of time in Big Squat's
basement, with its low crumbling ceiling that made
everyone crouch like a giant. 2: She stared at Herpes'
tattoos so intensely that when she would doodle
mindlessly, the tattoos were what would come out.

It was at a Hookworm68 concert where Claire met
Picasso. He was drinking an orange Tropical Fantasy,
the cheapest soda ever to exist, known more commonly
as "Sperm Killer." Picasso offered some to Claire and
she asked if he knew the soda's nickname. After that
they would say "Hi," which was a lot for Claire.

At one subpar Hookworm68 show, Picasso was
drinking something stronger than Sperm Killer.

He was drunk.

Claire was not, Claire was never.

She was barely 14, and along with anarchism and
Hookworm68, Claire was a fan of rebellion through
restraint. She didn't drink or smoke, she said please and
excuse me.

Hookworm68 had just closed their set with Claire's favorite song: "You Will End Up Dying of Comfort." Picasso sat down next to her and talked about the little dot on the underside of the tomato that no one ever ate. He was smiley and goofy and sweet and a little dull. It didn't seem possible that he could be 24 years old. He pulled a permanent marker from his jingle jacket and asked Claire to write on his head. Claire took the marker.

"Both sides or just one?" Claire asked.
"Both," Picasso answered, like that was obvious and implicit in the request.

Claire thought for a moment and then uncapped the marker with her teeth, which she regretted later.

"What did you write?" asked Picasso.
"I wrote 'Left' on one side and 'Right' on the other," Claire said—not sure if she had written it on her left or his.
"I'm glad you didn't write 'Empty,'" Picasso said, and then he asked Claire if she wanted to "go out."
"You mean to the bodega for chips?" Claire answered.
"No, like in a valentine way," Picasso said.

It was the first time Claire had ever been asked out on a date. She blushed: face, neck, and scalp. "Um no, no thanks," she said, and never wrote on Picasso's head again.

At Beggars, Monica used a database software called FileMaker Pro. It ran on Macs that were covered in band stickers. When one of Beggars' Macs broke, Monica was asked to take it to Tekserve.

She was smitten from the first foot in the door. The intaker noticed and said Tekserve was hiring.

Monica interviewed with both Dick and David at the same time. When they asked her what she wanted to do at Tekserve, she looked at their desks, covered in papers, and said it looked like they could use some help with that.

She was given a spot in their office. When David would turn around, her and Dick would snap rubber bands at each other in a joyous never-ending battle.

"If you want to get paid, listen to Monica," Patty tells Claire.
"Just listen to Monica," Monica simplifies.

The back of Tekserve is filled with workbenches. Patty leads Claire to the desktop repair area and introduces her to Derek, who has long dreadlocks and round cheeks.

Patty tells Claire he is her "go-to desktop tech," and that "he will let intake bug him nonstop." Derek pretends not to hear this. He is older than Patty and Claire. Before Tekserve, he was a music engineer. In the studio, he used Macs for MIDI sequencing.

Derek carved himself a spot recording R&B and hip hop artists he loved like Rakim and Mary J. Blige. But the work went late (all night) and was sporadic (at best). When his son turned 3 there was a reckoning.

He was hired as a full-fledged Tek after a short interview with Dick and then David. Derek's first day on the job, his very first repair was a Mac Plus with a broken floppy drive. He laid a towel out so he wouldn't scratch the screen, faced the Mac down and took off the case, exposing the floppy drive. He unscrewed the drive and started to slide it out.

Then he heard a hissing sound.

Shit, he thought, that's not good. Just at this moment Dick walked by. Derek asked Dick to listen.

"Is that bad?" Derek asked.

But in Derek's mind he knew it was bad.

He fucked up.

The Mac is super compact. He nicked a circuit board while sliding the floppy out. That circuit board was attached to the picture tube of the Mac's built-in monitor and he has cracked the tube. The hissing sound is proof. It is the sound of the tube's vacuum seal being broken. And he has ruined this Mac, and he was for sure supposed to know to pop that circuit board off before he slid the floppy drive out, and there is no way he is not going to be FIRED. He just hopes he doesn't need to pay for the picture tube.

"That is pretty bad," Dick said, "but don't worry about it. We always have old ones that we've bought from customers to use as parts. Just grab one off the shelf and try not to do it again."

Derek looked past Dick's lanky frame and saw a glowing shelf full of rescued parts. He never broke a picture tube again, but he used the glowing shelf all the time. If he thought a computer's problem was a bad processor, he'd go grab a good one from the shelf, and if the problem went away he would order a new processor for the machine and *boom*, move on to the next. If the problem didn't go away, he'd grab a logic board, and so on. This let him figure out the source of a machine's problem fast, which left him time to field questions from the steady stream of intakers like Patty.

"Deb is the best," Patty says as soon as they are out of Derek's earshot. Deb hears this and gives a small smile as she reassembles a gray laptop on her bench. She has hair even shorter than Claire's.

The Michigan hospital Deb was born in burned to the ground the day after she was delivered. She took this as a sign she was not meant for the Midwest.

In New York, Deb studied drama. After graduation, she worked a lighting board in a tiny magical theater at night and a day job so she could eat. The day job was at a private high school that had just bought brand new Macs for every classroom. Deb had only ever owned an electric typewriter, but she took to the Macs and became responsible for their well-being, which brought her to Tekserve.

This was around 1994. Tekserve was at its second location, the first location being Dick's loft. All versions of Tekserve were located on the north side of 23rd Street, between 6th and 7th Avenues, so that Dick could walk to work without even crossing a street.

This second Tekserve location was on the second floor of 163 23rd Street. Deb started to bring in the private school's Macs to be fixed or upgraded. At this time, Dick and David were both working the bench repairing computers. There was no intake station yet. You sat down with a technician and told them the problem. One day, Deb sat down with David to get some RAM installed in a PowerBook 500. In 1994, computers were slow. It could take fifteen minutes just for a computer to start. So they had time to talk.

After the repair, Deb got a call from David. "I know this is weird and maybe unorthodox, but would you like to work for us?" Deb said yes and became the first female technician at Tekserve. She also became the first Tek to specialize. She was tasked with fixing portable computers, since she had small, nimble hands.

As Deb worked at 163, more specialized technicians were added and intake was created. The Mac Plus was programmed to be a "now serving" machine and mounted above like a convenience store mirror. A billiard ball was hung on a string next to it, and was pulled to advance the serving numbers.

Customers came to the second floor depressed, clutching their ailing computers, to find a space that was as if Santa's workshop had made love to a Rube Goldberg machine, complete with mutated elves. Hearts would melt, Coca-Cola would flow from glass bottles, and customers would wait patiently for their number to be called.

Soon Tekserve outgrew 163 and moved a few doors down to the fourth floor of 155 23rd Street. Everything and everyone came along for the move, and it was the same, only more.

Deb places six tiny screws into the laptop's case, turns it over, and starts up the machine. She listens for the start-up bong. It sounds, and she reaches her small hand out to shake Claire's equally small hand. "Welcome to Tekserve," Deb says. "If you have portable questions, I will try to help . . . at least for your first intakes."

"Let's do it. Time is now," Patty says, and heads to the front of the loft. Claire trails behind her.

The intake area is made of plastic public school desks that wrap around the waiting area. There are fifteen intake stations, each with a laptop, half of them are being used. "64," Patty shouts, and waves her hand past a motion detector. The number on the Mac Plus above changes from 63 to 64. A couple holds up a ticket, and Patty calls them over.

Patty and Claire sit side by side at a laptop station. Ticket 64 sits across from them prison-visit style. The couple is young, max fifteen. Their eyes are dark, they hold hands, and only one speaks. And she can hardly speak. Her voice is soft, and her English is bad—very, very bad.

"They are sooo cute," Patty whispers in a spasm.

Patty shows Claire how to create an SRO in the Tekserve laptop. SRO stands for service repair order, and every intake needs one.

Ticket 64 hands Patty a PowerBook 1400, and signals that it won't start. Patty types notes in the SRO, signing them with her initials, PB. Patty communicates to the couple that she is going to take the laptop to do a few tests.

"It's probably that they need a new battery. Hardware issues are way easier than software issues," Patty says as she and Claire walk to a nearby bench. The bench is set up for intakers to test machines: SCSI adapters, a keyboard, a monitor, all types of power cords and batteries lie at the ready.

Patty flips the laptop over and points out a small plastic latch that will release the battery. She pushes the latch and starts to pull the battery from the machine.

A baby cockroach crawls out. Then another. Patty can see fifty more coming, so she shoves the battery back in fast. Claire automatically kills both baby roaches with her bare index finger.

"Oh no. What do I do? What do I do?" Patty says to Claire.

Claire says nothing. Derek walks by and Patty grabs him.

"Oh no. What do I do? What do I do?" Patty says again and again.

"You should ask David," Derek answers.

Claire holds her index finger up. It looks like she has an idea, but then she says, "I have to wash my finger."

They split up. Claire goes to the bathroom and Patty goes to David's office.

The problem is not hard at all for David. "You go back and tell them there are roaches inside the machine, and we can't fix it," David says.

"But it's not working, can't we do something?" Patty asks.
"NO, we can't. Get the roaches out of the facility. Tell them precisely what is going on."
"But they are adorable."

Patty hands the couple back the laptop. Their eyes get even bigger. She tells them roaches are living in it, and that Tekserve can't fix the machine.

The couple leaves. Patty looks like she will cry, but it passes. She tells Claire that it is important to write everything in the SRO. The computer serial number and customer will be linked to its history, and if the couple comes back, the next intaker will know the deal. Patty summarizes what happened in the notes field. She types *BIOHAZARD*, selects the text, and turns it red.

"Claire, this is important. If you pull up an SRO, and it fills the customer's name in purple, it means the customer was difficult. If you have an intake where the person is unbearably mean, lying, high-maintenance, or stone-cold crazy, put all your notes and the customer in the color purple. Purple = nightmare," Patty says, then stands, waves her hand, and calls for ticket 71.

71 is an older woman, she hobbles a little and carries a computer the shape of a pizza box.

"Have you been here before?" Patty asks.
"Yes, for software issues. But this is more serious. My computer is dead. I have work on it I need," she says.

Patty types in the woman's name, and the SRO fills with her contact info set in black type.

The woman's name is Harriet. She has had a hard day: the machine, an LC 4500, would not power on, and when she went to unplug the LC, she stubbed her toe so bad it bled. Patty takes notes in the SRO, or nods her head with concern. Harriet is a scientist up at Columbia University, her life is on this machine, and it is not backed up.

"I'm just going to take it to the back, to our bench, and have a Tek look at it. If you do need data recovery, it is expensive and not guaranteed, but this problem seems to me like it is unrelated to the hard drive." Patty says this with softness, picking up the computer. She and Claire head to Derek's bench.

Claire went to Columbia for a semester.

She took as many philosophy classes as possible. One of the classes was Existentialism 101. The professor had a thick accent that made it even harder to comprehend the human condition. What little Claire did understand between the rolled "r"s was earth-shattering. The professor loved nihilism and it was infectious. But his accent thickened with every class.

The situation was made worse by his habit of teaching through asking questions.

"What dew whe ate most?" the professor asked.
"Instant ramen," a student called out.
"And why dew whe all ate onstant ramon?" the prof asked.
"It is cheap," another student replied.
"But what whe really ate is, maybe, ourselves, that we kon't offord more than ramon."

And the class all at once realized the professor was asking about "hate," not what they "ate."

Students started to withdraw. The class shrunk to eight people, who all seemed to be fluent in French.

Claire realized she had to stop going.

It was easy to drop the class, she had never signed up for it in the first place.

She wasn't enrolled at Columbia.

She had never even applied.

Claire would go up and sit in on classes as a hobby. The fewer the students in the class, the more likely it was she would get caught.

The hobby started when Claire found a Columbia student ID on the sidewalk. If the ID could come all the way downtown why couldn't Claire go all the way up? It was a voyage to the moon.

Black iron gates opened to a perspective drawing of green lawns and white columns. Students sat in circles under sun-dappled light. The air was clean and weightless. Shadows were not cast from skyscrapers but from sundials, sculptures, and sycamore trees. Paths and quads crisscrossed to neoclassical buildings with doors that swung wide open. It didn't feel anything like New York City. There were public restrooms everywhere.

Claire decided not to return the ID.

She studied the giant enameled campus map, squinting, unaccustomed to such an abundance of light. Wedged between buildings named for humans like Schermerhorn, Avery, Kent, and Mudd was a building named for thought.

Claire made a beeline to the building.

A huge sculpture of Rodin's *Le Penseur* (a.k.a *The Thinker*) greeted her. She stared up at him, his giant cheese-doodle toes curled in concentration, and deemed the bronze's placement a bit too on the nose.

PHILOSOPHY was affixed to the building in cast capital letters. Claire bounded up the steps flanked by ornamental shrubs, empowered by the found ID in her pocket.

Inside, the building felt normal. It was a relief. Classroom desks were the same as at Claire's public school, the plastic-one-armed-mailbox-flag-looking things with chrome legs and disc feet.

The stair landing had a beat-up bulletin board covered in staples and torn corners with a lone flyer that read:

FAIL HARDER
Samuel Beckett dissected – Instructor: Sarah Adams
Thursdays 6 p.m.–8 p.m.
(visit room 310 for more information)

Claire visited room 310. She found a stack of free booklets that listed all the classes offered by the philosophy department. The staple-bound pages had detailed descriptions and course codes, but most important, they listed when and where the classes were held. One was starting in an hour. Claire went to the student store and bought a notebook and a light blue Columbia pencil.

In her Tek interview when David asked if she was "mechanical," the Columbia ID was the first thing Claire thought of. How she had replaced the photo and name with her own. The epic search for the right lamination kit and date sticker. And the foresight she had shown in making a second ID with a fake name to cover all her bases.

The ID was legit enough to get her into the library and anywhere else she had tried. Including an orange-colored student dorm that to her surprise contained no woodwork, chandeliers, or fireplaces. The dorm was a twin of a budget hotel save for its grand piano and the long line of students waiting to play it.

Claire never got busted. She began working full-time, and the moon suddenly seemed too far away from where she lived.

"This just needs a new PRAM battery," Derek says, and Patty smiles. The repair is twelve dollars, which is the cost of the battery. The battery looks like a miniature soda can. It will be replaced in under a half hour, while Harriet waits, and all her data will be just fine.

Patty shows Claire how to intake the machine proper, printing the SRO and taping it to Harriet's LC.

"78," Patty calls out.

Ticket 78 is a man named Jerry with a beard and an original Mac Plus. Patty starts an SRO. Jerry apologizes, he knows the computer is old, but just the mouse is broken. He places the beige one-button box on the desk and explains that it won't scroll left or right—up and down are fine. "We have a few people who can fix this. Let me take the mouse to the back and see if I can find one," Patty says, scooping the mouse up. She leads Claire past the desktops and portable benches to a little alley piled high with massive monitors.

"LYUBEN, this is Claire," Patty says. Lyuben has gray hair interrupted by a gray plastic headband with a pair of magnifying glasses attached. He flips the lenses up and looks hello at Patty and Claire.

Lyuben is ageless, in that he is so old it is hard to say just how old he is. Patty shows him the mouse and says, "No work." She moves her finger up and down. Then she crosses her arms in an X. Lyuben takes the mouse and puts it on his workbench. Lyuben was born in Bulgaria. As soon as he had a lap, there was an accordion in it. He is old enough to have crisp memories of surviving World Wars I and II.

The memories are hard to hear. Lyuben speaks thirteen languages—Bulgarian, Russian, French, but he doesn't care to count English in that number. "Bulgarian every word has just one meaning. One letter, one sound," Lyuben will explain, his small arsenal of English reserved solely for its resistance.

Before he came to America, Lyuben was the head of BNR's folk music station (BNR = Bulgarian National Radio). He loved the job that combined his talent and obsession, and included a summer dacha. Then he met a girl. She was a musician, too, but her passion was to go to America.

They married and moved to New York, sure that Lyuben would find work as a musician. He did not. The only job he could find was operating a freight elevator, so he took it. Soon his marriage split up, but they shared a daughter.

Lyuben didn't really make money from concerts, but he played them in the evenings wherever he could. One night a man named Ed was in the audience. Ed was stunned by Lyuben—by his music, by his playing, by his spirit, but also by how shitty his day gig was.

Ed offered Lyuben a job at the company he managed. The company was Acoustiguide. It was soon learned Lyuben was an electronics whiz. He had been a radio operator for the army in the war and had built the first superheterodyne receiver in Bulgaria. Whatever that was, everyone realized he was a better fit for Current Designs.

Lyuben began on the tape players that Current Designs sold to Acoustiguide. When that died down, he repaired power supplies of the Mac Plus, then graduated to working on anything Dick or David asked him to fix at Tekserve, mostly at this moment CRT monitors.

Lyuben flips his magnifying glasses down and opens the plastic case of the mouse.

When Claire was a kid, her family lived in an old building that seemed magic. It was as though the fountain of youth lay between the walls and floors, but replace the word "youth" with "mice."

It was a problem.

Yellow rectangles hugged the perimeter of the apartment and anything else they could: socked feet, Matchbox cars, spilled beans, a lazy cat, and lots and lots of mice. When a glue trap traps a mouse it is caught alive. The mouse is stuck writhing, trying to escape or accepting its lot but wanting to get a bit more comfortable.

Both realities were awful.

The two fates freaked out Claire's mom. But it freaked her mom out even more to throw a live mouse away. To have it wriggling in the garbage can, where she imagined it might eat so much that its mouse muscles would swell mighty like a snake's body.

Faced with watching the mice starve for days or drowning them quick, Claire's mom found a compromise: she put the caught mice in the freezer.

But Claire's mom would forget about the mouse as soon as the freezer door shut.

Claire would go in for a Creamsicle and there would always be one or two or five frozen dead mice. They were right beside the lumpy bag of peas that was kept and reused for falls, bumped heads, and once to soothe Claire's brother's bloody earlobe after he pierced it with an embroidery needle.

Even though she instinctively blurred her sight as a defense upon opening the freezer, Claire had recurring nightmares about a mouse hiding in her Hot Pocket, somehow surviving the microwave.

The frozen mice scared her, until they didn't. One day, she grabbed a paper towel, and with no fear threw a frost-covered gray blob away. It became her family chore. After school, first foot in the door she would check the icebox.

Claire did this until her family switched from glue traps to the wooden ones with a spring and a slice of plastic baited with peanut butter.

The peanut butter traps caught even more mice than the glue traps. But there was no need for the freezer, the snap of the spring killed the mice without fail.

It was more gruesome, but also more humane. Given the choice of death, Claire would choose the peanut butter trap in a heartbeat.

The cord is a quarter inch shorter, but the beige mouse is no longer trapped. The repair is deemed a special case and the charge for the mouse is goodwill.

The intake stations are all manned, and the waiting room is full. Patty instructs Claire to wave her hand and call out the number. "Ticket 85," Claire says softly.

"TICKET 85," Patty shouts, correcting Claire.

It is 8:30 a.m. on the dot. Bagels, smoked salmon and sable, lettuce, tomatoes on the vine, fresh squeezed juice, coffee, melons, strawberries, oysters, sea urchins sliced open with soft orange insides, croissants, ham, French cheese, hard-boiled eggs, and caviar cascade with ripe beauty and grace across the Formica table of the Tekserve kitchen.

Patty introduces Claire to Dick, the cofounder of Tekserve, who is washing grapes. Dick encourages Claire to eat.

"This happens every Thursday. It gets us all to come on time. Dick buys everything across the street at Garden of Eating. The spread is always bonkers," Patty says, sliding an oyster down her throat.

Claire has never seen an oyster. She doesn't share this fact. Patty introduces her to the other employees: a giantess from Venezuela named Diana; Anthony, who wears a hoodie and works data recovery; a man with a red nose named Gary; and twenty more.

"I forgot to introduce Lisa," Patty says, and pulls Claire toward Thor and Monica's office.

Lisa is seven inches long and covered in spots. She is a leaf cichlid, a.k.a. leopard bush fish.

"Lisa has a lot of personality—like so much she doesn't get along with other fish," Patty says as she gazes at the fish who, no joke, gazes back. "She basically has killed anybody that Dick put in the tank. I think she killed an electric eel."

Gary comes up beside Patty, and Lisa switches her stare to him. Gary bobs his head and Lisa follows. Their eyes are locked. Patty steps back from the tank. Claire never really stepped forward. Gary tilts left, and Lisa follows. Then he tilts right, and she does, too. He leads her up and down. Lisa picks up speed and starts to somehow growl. She goes back and forth in the tank, leading Gary left and right.

There is a splash and then another. The smile falls from Gary's face. Lisa churns as though she is turning cream to butter. Quarts of water escape her tank on all sides. To the right of her tank is a big trash can; to the left is a laser printer the same size as the trash can but worth ten thousand dollars.

A gush of water hits the laser printer right in the kisser.

There is a moment of silence.

The printer is pronounced dead. Dick isn't angry.

Really.

He is fascinated by the event and excited to improve the cover for Lisa's tank.

Claire calls out ticket 97 and sits down next to Patty.

The tickets don't start fresh each day. Every time the
red machine at the door dispenses a ticket, it signals
this fact to a computer, so numbers are called only if a
ticket was given out.

They blast through intakes. Claire learns about Apple
warranties, system software installs, bad ports, and data
recovery.

"If a machine's drive is clicking, shut it off. Every
second the computer is on, the customer's data can be
lost. If there is a reco issue, don't start the machine."
Patty continues, "The way data reco works is Tekserve
clones the customer's failing drive to a new healthy hard
drive. After that, file by file, bit by bit, Tek recovers
the data that has been left for dead. We charge for a
new drive and the specialized labor. It takes a lot of
time. I encourage people to just move on and accept it
as fate, but that is not what most people choose to do."

Data reco is a dark art. When Patty says "Tekserve"
does all this, she means Anthony, the dude in the
hoodie that rode a skateboard to work from Rego Park
and is taking a smoke break on the fire escape right
now.

No other shop in New York does data recovery. The service barely exists. There are experts in California that charge fifteen hundred dollars a drive. They operate from a clean room with a staff that wears bunny suits and enters through air locks.

Anthony once recovered a screenplay from William Goldman's dead drive. Goldman sent a gift basket for the whole staff, and insisted on treating David (a hard-core vegetarian) to a meal at the jacket-required restaurant Daniel. Columbia professors, animators, novelists, rappers, artists, designers, and more rappers have had their heart broken to pieces and put back together by Anthony in about a week for around six hundred dollars.

Patty and Claire swap places. Claire asks the customers if they have been to Tekserve before and types notes in SROs signed with her own initials. She brings laptop after laptop to Deb and desktop after desktop to Derek.

Claire's fingers stretch across a customer's keyboard in Tekserve's gang sign. She presses down command-option-P-R and waits until the machine's start-up sound repeats three times.

The P-ram is zapped. Which is code for resetting the parameter RAM, the part of the computer that stores its core character—the sounds it makes, its preferences, its conception of time, its habits good and bad.

Patty gives Claire a last bit of advice. "If you don't know something, don't make like you do. David's cardinal rule is: Assumption is the mother of all fuckups."

"Ticket 53," Claire yells. A man with a hand truck full of iMacs stands up and wheels them over to her. He unstraps red and blue bungee cords that hold the grape, lime, strawberry, and tangerine iMacs together. Claire asks which of the computers is broken. Ticket 53 answers, "All of them."

Claire starts an SRO and asks 53 his name. "Jim Munster," he says. She types it in, and it pops up in purple.

The intaker sitting next to Claire is named Jeffrey. Skinny and neat with gray hair, he worked at WBAI with Dick and David way, way back. After WBAI, Jeffrey ended up working at what was known as the WBAI graveyard: Acoustiguide. He began selling the audio guides door to door, and worked his way into the office.

In early 1985, Jeffrey took a vacation. He went to Hawaii to visit a friend named Sam, who owned a retreat. The first thing Sam said to Jeffrey (lei around his neck and suitcase still in hand) was, "You've got to see this." Sam led Jeffrey up a huge hill to a gorgeous redwood octagon shrine flanked by birds-of-paradise and elephant ears. Inside, the windows were made of mosquito nets that acted as Vaseline on the lens, revealing in soft focus the beaches, skies, and mountains of Maui, while the scent of eucalyptus wafted through the mesh.

Sam pulled Jeffrey away from the window toward a beige box. A tone sounded, disk drives whished and whirred in what Jeffrey remembers as a magic elixir.

And that is how Jeffrey met his first Mac.

It hurt to want something so bad and know he couldn't afford it.

When Jeffrey got back from Hawaii, he found, in his office, the same magic beige box.

Current Designs had convinced Acoustiguide that they had to buy a Mac. It would save them tons of money, and it was the future.

A printer was added. Now the scripts for the tours that Acoustiguide recorded could be changed and printed instantly.

Jeffrey became Acoustiguide's creative director and a total Mac fanatic. He had tried to use computers before the Mac, especially WordStar on DOS, but he was dyslexic and he couldn't learn the commands. It just wasn't how his brain was wired.

He spent more than a decade at Acoustiguide. The company was sold multiple times. One of the new owners hired a consultant to talk to all the employees. Jeffrey kept a photo of his boyfriend on his desk.

The new owner said it was okay for Jeffrey to be gay but not to talk about it, and with that Jeffrey was let go.

Tekserve hired Jeffrey on a trial basis. This was because, 1: David didn't really like him, and 2: He wasn't a tech wizard.

Jeffrey started at Tek's second location, on the second floor.

It felt good to be in a place with a Coke machine again. At WBAI, the machine was the center of the station. Jeffrey remembered the first time he was privileged to fill the machine. It was then he learned that all the Coke was stockpiled from Passover because kosher Coke had pure cane sugar rather than corn syrup.

At Tekserve, all the employees were made of pure cane sugar, not corn syrup. Jeffrey fit the bill, and his trial period was put to an end.

One day, a Bondi blue iMac was dropped off under warranty. Tekserve had moved up the block, and by this time Jeffrey was the den mother of intake. When Eli, the desktop tech, opened the blue iMac, a clear gel blanketed its inside all the way down to the logic board. Eli was used to spills. Beer, tea, cat vomit, but he had never seen a spill like this before. He called the owner named John, and said the repair wouldn't be covered under Apple's warranty. He explained that the machine was damaged from a spill.

John lost his shit and came straight to Tekserve.

Eli pointed out to John the three parentheses on top of the iMac where the goo likely entered, and opened the machine, revealing its slimy innards.

John screamed that the spill must have happened at Tekserve, that the mystery goo dripped down while the iMac was waiting to be repaired. He wanted to see the exact spot the computer was stored.

The screaming brought Jeffrey over. He took one look at the goo.

"This is WET," Jeffrey said to John, who went quiet.

"You know what that is. It is a sex lube, and there is no way it came from Tekserve. Some trick, for heaven knows why, poured it in your machine on purpose. This is not under warranty, and we are not at fault." Jeffrey said this as fact, and it was.

John grabbed the sticky computer and huffed out the door.

Jeffrey knew Jim Munster was purple. Jim and a rabbi with an overclocked processor were the inspiration for flagging customers. Jim made his living by buying open-boxed, as-is, lemon computers that were still under warranty. He would get them repaired and resell them at a profit. But that's not what put him in purple. He was purple at the dentist and supermarket. Jim was always difficult, and it had nothing to do with the reality of the situation. It was born from childhood trauma, or hard luck, or a heart of darkness. Whatever the cause, Jim was the very definition of purple.

"Claire honey, you're new, let me do this intake for you. You can delete the SRO," Jeffrey says, and points at the chair opposite him.

Jim Munster and his purple aura switch seats. Claire relaxes, smiles thanks at Jeffrey, and calls out for ticket 55.

Ticket 55 has long arms that hug a laptop to her flat chest. She sits down with her hair in a tight bun and wonderful posture that is the opposite of Claire's.

Claire recognizes the woman. Claire's dad once pointed number 55 out on their block. He said she was a prima ballerina and went on to explain that being a ballerina was a raw deal. The dance companies demanded all their time, broke all their bones, and only wanted them young. He said 55 hadn't had any kind of life till she was let go from the company at age 22. She hadn't even kissed a boy till she was 23. But in the end it worked out okay. Though he was the only boy she'd ever kissed, they fell in love, got married, and were together still.

Claire knew her father was making it up, but she clung to the story.

55's laptop just needs a new battery. Claire sells her a generic one that Tekserve stocks. The battery is seventy dollars cheaper than the Apple version.

By free lunch on Wednesday, it is easier for Claire to diagnose and estimate a repair than to figure out which burrito she wants.

It is hard not to cut people off when they describe their problems.

But cutting people off is not the Tekserve way. Patty taught this Tao well, and Claire abides, listening to every tangent and tragedy that has befallen each computer's owner.

Claire zips through tickets, mindful of the Tao. It is a surprise when David calls her into the area that is his office.

David, with no shoes and the diskette line floating above, asks Claire how she likes intake.

Claire replies that she is just getting the hang of it, to which David asks if she would like to become a printer technician. This surprises Claire even more than being called into the office.

"But I don't have any training," Claire says.
"We can train you. It's not rocket science. You can do it. It's a promotion," David says, making it clear she was supposed to just say yes.

"Then yes, I want to become a printer technician," Claire says.
"Great. You can start training now. Joel . . . have you met Joel?"
"No. I haven't, um. I haven't had to intake a printer yet."
"Oh," David pauses. "Well, Joel will train you, but he leaves in a week."
"Okay. Will I be the only printer tech?"
"No, Gary has been training with Joel for a month. But we need another tech."

David leads Claire to the printer bench, which is just beyond the staff kitchen, and introduces her to Joel.

"You are proper young," Joel says, shaking Claire's hand with his hair flopping and accent exposed. He was born in São Paulo, Brazil, and has a baby and a wife.

He went to Berklee. Not the Berkeley in California. He went to the Berklee College of Music in Boston, where he studied music production and met his first Mac. Out of school, he got the dream internship, the one that the "entire university wanted to get." It was at a recording studio located in Chelsea, not far from Tekserve.

It turned out to be a nightmare. He was a runner, getting coffee, and helping with everything except making music. There was no pay and long hours.

Joel took one of the recording studio's Macs to get fixed. He fell in love with Tekserve and asked for a job, but they weren't hiring.

Joel quit the dream job. He applied at Banana Republic, the Gap, and McDonald's for work. No one hired him. His heart throbbed to work at Tekserve. He went back and begged. This time they said yes. He was hired for intake.

A month in, Dick sat all of the intake workers down for reeducation. Dick held up two SROs, one that was an example of a good intake and one that was an example of a bad one.

Dick didn't dwell on who had made them. But everyone knew because they were signed. The good one was by DDQ, a.k.a. Diana. The bad was by JVL, a.k.a. Joel. An opening came to do printer repair and Joel jumped at it.

So many musicians worked at Tekserve. After work they would all get together and practice. Joel played guitar. There were drummers and singers and bassists, enough for a softball team. Derek got the team a paying music gig once a week. Joel's heart and wallet were happy.

Before Joel knew it, his visa was set to expire. He needed a sponsor, so he asked Dick. Dick said yes, but when Joel and his wife talked to a lawyer they found out it would cost ten thousand dollars, and they wouldn't be able to leave the country for four to five years.

They decided it wasn't worth it and that they would move to London. They were flying there in a week and a half. The tickets were already booked.

Behind Joel are shelves full of printers with SROs taped to their fronts—printers made by Hewlett-Packard, Xerox, and Brother, but most of all by Apple. This is despite the fact Apple doesn't make printers anymore.

Apple's first printer was announced in 1979. It was called the Apple Silentype and was a thermal printer that used heat-sensitive paper rather than ink.

The Silentype was based on another manufacturer's design, a Trendcom model 200. The Apple version looked exactly like the 200. Same shape, size, and shit-brown color. But inside, the circuit board was redesigned. Apple removed the microprocessor and memory, handing the computing work off to the software. This allowed Apple to sell the printer at a lower cost, while still keeping print quality high.

It was a bargain at $699. The printer was more reliable than dot-matrix printers with their fussy carriages, and it was quieter and half the size. There was a rumor Woz kept one under the seat of his private plane. Customers fell in love with the printer the same way they did with their Macs.

In 1985, Apple produced their first laser printer, the LaserWriter (later known as LaserWriter I). Apple didn't make the first consumer laser printer, they made the fourth, after IBM, Xerox, and HP. The LaserWriter used the same exact Canon engine as the HP LaserJet, but the LaserWriter was better. It featured new software that Jobs had invested 2.5 million dollars in called Adobe PostScript. PostScript was a wonder. It compressed images, shapes, and fonts into seeds that were sent to the LaserWriter, which then bloomed into razor-sharp type at any point size, perfect Bézier curves and halftones, all printed at blazing speed in an archival ink. The LaserWriter was the death of dot matrix and the birth of desktop publishing. It cost $6,995 and was worth every cent.

Joel grabs an HP LaserJet from the shelf and puts it on the bench. "Don't trust what the intake describes. Make sure you see the problem yourself," Joel says, connecting the printer to the laptop on his bench.

The printer jams immediately, just as the SRO said it would. Joel points out the error lights. One is solid red, another flashes on and off with an amber glow.

Joel tells Claire she can decode the lights by checking three places. The first is HP's technical manual. The second is message boards. And the last place is the best place. It is Tekserve's own PRINTER FAQ.

Joel opens the FAQ and looks up the model of LaserJet. There, splayed out in plain spoke, spiked with tiny jokes, is all the ways a LaserJet ever broke.

Joel straps a purple bracelet around his wrist that has a coiled cord connected to the bench. Claire asks what it is for, and Joel explains that it grounds him, preventing him from making static electricity that might fry the circuit board. He says anytime you are near a machine's insides you have to wear one. Claire hadn't noticed it before, but now she can't unsee that every Tek has a blue or purple bracelet on.

Joel starts to undress the printer, slipping its beige plastic off in a magic trick. Then he puts the case back on and shows Claire how he did it. Plastic tabs are bent slightly till they unlatch. Claire is warned that they are easy to break, and she shouldn't push too hard or the whole case will need to be replaced. Joel goes deeper into the printer, warning Claire at every step. The screws are tiny and easy to lose. Wires must be tucked back neatly lest they block the paper's path.

The problem is the gear assembly. This is a part that helps turn the rollers in rhythm to feed the paper through. A tooth has broken off.

Joel shows Claire where the parts are kept and what part numbers are and how to restock them, and everything is signed with initials and everything requires knowing the thing before.

The gear assembly looks like a Spirograph set. Joel unscrews it and hands it to Claire to inspect. She caresses the part, spinning its dysfunctional gears. Claire asks if the broken part gets recycled. When Joel answers that it will go in the trash, she asks if she can keep it. Joel laughs and says of course she can.

After the gear assembly is replaced, Joel replaces the LaserJet's fan. The PRINTER FAQ told him to do this because the fan (much like capitalism) has a design flaw that makes it eventually fail, and as long as you are all the way deep in the printer you should replace it. The FAQ also says if the fan is the thing that fails, you should preemptively replace the gear assembly because one of its gears is prone to having teeth break off.

Joel says the worst thing on earth is to fix a printer and have it come back within the year broken again. Claire feels this truth in her bones.

The LaserJet is put back together, and a hundred test pages are printed. The hundred pages are made of a waterfall of type that espouses Tekserve's core values:

This Is a Test Print From Tekserve - Old Reliable Mac Repair - Honest Weights Square

Dealings. This Is a Test Print From Tekserve - Old Reliable Mac Repair - Honest Weights Square Dealings. This Is a Test Print From Tekserve - Old Reliable Mac Repair - Honest Weights Square Dealings. This Is a Test Print From Tekserve - Old Reliable Mac Repair - Honest Weights Square Dealings. This Is a Test Print From Tekserve - Old Reliable Mac Repair - Honest Weights Square Dealings. This Is a Test Print From Tekserve - Old Reliable Mac Repair - Honest Weights Square Dealings.

Claire asks if it isn't a waste of toner to print so many pages? Joel reminds her of the worst thing on earth.

Gary comes back from lunch surprised. No one told him Claire was training. His round face twists up so gnarly that his beard can't even hide it. The twisting stops and lands on a toothy smile. He extends his hand to Claire and says, "Welcome to the printer bench." Gary keeps talking—it is a flood of things, tips about the phone system, tips about solenoids and pick-up rollers. None of it makes sense to Claire.

Joel laughs. This stops Gary from talking.

Joel asks Gary if he can handle the phones for the afternoon while Claire is being trained. Gary says, "On it, chief." And on cue, the phone rings. Gary goes to his bench and picks up the call.

"Part of printer repair is answering Tek support calls," Joel says, and tells Claire he will teach her that tomorrow. Then his voice drops to below a whisper, and he says, "Don't listen to Gary about printers." He says it so fast and low, Claire wonders if she imagined it.

An intaker named Chaz plops a medium-size laser printer on Joel's bench.

"The paper tray sticks like a mofo. The owner says the printer prints great, but the drawer is driving her totally nuts. Can you take a look at it now? If you can't, just tell me what I should quote for?" Chaz adds the last part as protocol. Joel already has hands on the plastic latch of the drawer.

A shrill scraping squeal sounds as Joel yanks it open.

"That sound, again. It always comes at THE worst time," says a tiny spring within the printer.
"What? What? Sorry I couldn't hear you!" shouts a gray roller.

The spring hesitates, making sure the sound has fully stopped.

It has.

The spring twists open, but the sound starts just as she begins to speak. This makes the gray roller laugh. Tiny spring is upset for a second but then begins to lip-synch her little lips to the giant sound.

"Stop, stop," the gray roller says, spinning uncontrollably with laughter. The spring starts dancing, perfectly matching the high notes of the screeching with her hips.

Gray roller sheds tears of joy and dreams of having hands to slap his round knee.

The sound stops.

The spring slumps. "But really, we must do something about the sound. I fear it."

The gray roller begins to rock in a soothing way. "I hated it at first, but now it is just part of life. Take heart, don't get too wound up. Try to focus on the fact that the sound is always followed by fresh, crisp sheets that feel as if they were dried in the sun and radiate fresh air upon us."

"But it seems to be getting worse, it is louder and louder and has happened five times in a row with no new sheets," the tiny spring says, bouncing up and down.

This catches gray roller off guard. But he recovers: "Sometimes it must get worse before it gets better."

Joel grabs a silver tube from his bench and shows Claire how to grease the track of the tray. He slides the tray in and out, distributing the grease till it glides silently with ease.

"It's a no-charge repair. Tek doesn't sell silicone grease, but the customer should try to buy some because the squeaking might come back in a few months," Joel says to Chaz, and adds, "Have you met Claire? She's the new printer Tek."

Claire turns red and gives a little wave, which is less a wave than an easy way to get her hand to her forehead to cover her eyes.

The printer's bench is a box seat to the staff kitchen. Patty was right. This Thursday's spread is somehow more bonkers than it was the week before. Bing cherries spill forth, taut as dilated pupils. A hulk of a UPS delivery man helps himself to a plate crowded with a blueberry muffin, salami, quiche, and chocolate-covered strawberries.

"That's Vito," Joel says, noticing Claire noticing the man dressed in trademark brown. "He takes good care of Tekserve, never makes us come down to the truck for parts. And Tekserve takes proper care of him," Joel says, laughing.

A rush has started, and the spread is being decimated. All the seats around the table are taken.

Winnie is younger than Claire by two years, but looks more adult, with long black hair and a mouth that opens to speak now and then. She is a newbie intaker and is sitting next to Deb and Yee. Yee is a desktop Tek who studied opera in college and is the opposite of a newbie.

On Yee's first day at Tekserve, he was given an employee handbook that concluded with the statement, "If you are ever in doubt, do the right thing." He had just quit a job that was at the other end of the moral spectrum. The job was designing inventory systems for a consortium of Persian rug and wedding gown dealers. Everybody in the office was three times Yee's age and, for whatever reason, they all ate kidney beans for lunch. So it was just people smoking and farting all day and arguing about rug and lace prices. Yee lasted just shy of a week.

When he landed at Tek, there was no intake. He was hired as a technician, though he had previously only worked with software. The bench Yee took had belonged to an employee named Boris who had recently overdosed. A program for his funeral was tacked above as Yee set to fixing a Power Macintosh 8500. David had given him the computer's manual and some basic tips. Yee spent the whole day on it, but he got it done, and when he went home, he thought to himself, "This is the job I was born to do."

Deb struggles to eat a Danish, her wrist in a cast. Yee asks Deb how she broke it, wondering if it was tennis or a fall.

"Masturbating," Deb says.

The staff table erupts. Winnie's eyes bulge, she blushes, gulps down her orange juice, and starts to leave. On the way out, she bumps into Gary.

"Shall we dance?" Gary says, and bows. Winnie smiles and gives a tiny curtsy, her face returning to its normal soft yellow.

Stragglers peck at the breakfast shards. One has bushy eyebrows and wears a suit with a tie and cuff links. Nobody at Tekserve wears a suit, not even the customers.

"Nathan," Joel calls out, and the suit walks over to the printer bench.

"I hear you are escaping," Nathan says, bagel in hand. Joel laughs, but his eyes water and he swallows hard at the thought of it. "I want you to meet Claire," Joel says, turning toward thin air.

Claire is no longer next to Joel. She has hauled ass to the far end of the bench and taken refuge in a LaserJet. This doesn't faze Joel. He leads Nathan over to her and reboots.

"I want you to meet Claire. She is the newest printer tech," Joel continues. "And Claire, meet Nathan. He was the printer Tek before me."

Claire shakes Nathan's hand. The coiled cord of her antistatic bracelet is still attached and bounces in soft waves.

"That's smart. We would have made sparks and melted your motherboard," Nathan says with a smile, his eyes fixed on Claire's pink lips.

Claire unsnaps the cord from her bracelet and takes a few steps back.

"Let me see your wrist. I think the bracelet is too big for you," Nathan says. Claire holds her wrist up and Nathan brings his nose toward it. "Yeah, you definitely should tighten it," he says.
"It's as tight as it can go. Is it okay?" Claire asks.
"Well, it is probably fine then. Maybe just try to push it up your forearm."
Claire pushes the bracelet halfway to her elbow, and Nathan nods approval.

"If you have printer questions, Nathan is the best person to ask. I will be asleep and across an ocean," Joel says.

"Yeah, just leave me a message, and I'll try to stop by." Nathan pauses for a moment and continues, "I don't really talk on the phone."

"I'm training Claire on phones today if you want a lesson?" Joel says, and laughs.

"It doesn't ring that often, but if you're deep in the muck, take it off the hook. Just slightly," Joel says, and positions the handset of the phone askew in the cradle.

Joel puts the phone back to normal, and it immediately rings. "Printers," Joel says, picking up the call.

The caller's printer won't take paper in. Claire listens as Joel tells the caller how to use some Scotch tape to clean the machine's pick-up rollers, giving them a little more life. When the call is over, he shows Claire how to do it, pressing the tape against the rubber rollers of a LaserJet and then peeling it off like he is waxing a woman's mustache. As he displays the tape covered in dust and squiggles, Joel warns it is just a trick to help callers. He explains if a pick-up roller is dirty or bald, it needs to be replaced, and all the exposed rollers need to be checked.

Claire asks how to bill for the calls. Joel tells her not to, that it is 100% free, a goodwill thing. In the eyes of Dick and David, anything that makes a Mac user happy is good for Tekserve.

Joel describes a call he had once. It lasted an hour. A woman couldn't get her computer and printer synced. Finally they got the machines paired. When he told her there was no charge, she couldn't believe it. A week later, the woman came to Tekserve in person, all the way to Joel's bench just to thank him.

Joel's eyes well a bit at his own story. He recovers quick with a few laughs and tells Claire to pick a printer off the shelf.

In a Frankenstein walk, Claire hauls a LaserWriter II to the bench. It is an elegant forty-five-pound beast of a thing cloaked in a gray color called "Platinum." The case is cut with parallel lines for form and function. Claire remembers rubbing these stripes as a kid, her fingers always ending on the rainbow of the embedded domed Apple logo.

"Not this SRO. Man, this is the worst repair. Absolute. And once you start, you can't stop," Joel says.

"Oh, okay," Claire replies, but then continues, her voice even smaller, "Um, the thing is, I need to learn how to fix it. And it is the printer that has been here the longest."

Joel looks at his wristwatch and nods okay.

Joel explains that the LaserWriter II was discontinued almost ten years ago. But Tek always encourages people to fix them. Always. LaserWriter IIs are tanks, one of the most solid printers Apple ever made. The printer has only one design flaw, one thing that consistently breaks, and that flaw takes ten years to surface. Joel pauses for breath. Claire is on the edge of her seat.

He concludes, "The fan blades warp a little over time and suck in dust. This dust eventually gets into the optics and causes pages to ghost."

Claire prints a test page from the LaserWriter II. The edges of the paper are bright white. They stipple to a black stripe of text in the center, in a kind of reverse ice cream sandwich.

Ghosting is a term used to cover a host of printing problems—double images, an image seen through the backside of the paper. Here Joel uses "ghost" to describe printing so faint it has not actually printed.

"I hate this repair. You have to take the whole thing apart. Vacuum and wipe the dust all the way bloody down," Joel says, pulling out a tan vacuum with a trolley of attachments and a long hose.

A hook and gear gaze in wonder as particles fly through the air.

"What is happening?" asks the hook.
"I don't know, but it is beautiful. I've never seen anything like this," replies the gear.
"Well, I have. All the damn time," says the lower fan, who has been eavesdropping from below. The gear and hook look at each other and mouth the word ASSHOLE.

"Are you cold?" asks the hook, noticing that the gear's teeth are chattering.
"No, just that strange hum is making me shake." The gear adds, "You should know that you are doing it, too."

And sure enough, the hook saw that he was shaking ever so slightly. So was the floor, the screws, and the DC controller. Even the I/O board was vibrating.

"The dust is being taken away," hook said, trying to point with his knuckle.
The gear began to cry.
"I watched that dust grow, it kept me warm."
"Yeah . . . but maybe a little too warm?"
"No, just-right warm. I don't want it to go."
And the gear's teeth chattered, not just from the alien hum, but from terror.

"Hey dude, calm down," begged the hook.

"NO. I don't want the dust to go. I'm scared, and now I am very, very cold," wailed the gear.

From the deep beyond came a willowy sound. At first the hook and gear thought it was a theremin, that the visiting vibration had brought with it a steady oscillation and somehow the shaking of the cotter pins and levers was altering the pitch to play a kind of spooky music. This was a very complicated thought to have at the same time. It soon proved to be totally wrong.

"You must not be scared," the willowy sound that was actually a voice said. Hook then realized it was the voice of the octagonal mirror that directed the laser's raw beam. She was speaking from within the scanner assembly above.

"You must not be scared, ponder Nietzsche's thoughts of eternal recurrence. Imagine this life you live now, you have lived before. Life is a loop that repeats infinitely and exactly. Every pain and pleasure shall return to you. Do you want to be a coward immortal? Think of the kidnapping of the dust as when Herr Friedrich shook off a decade of moss by visiting the Cave of Mithras. Imagine this moment as a seminal visit to the island of Capri . . . Does that help?" asks the octagonal mirror.

There is a long silence.

"So you think it is a good thing?" says hook.

Octagonal mirror's voice wavers in reply, "As Susan Sontag said, 'Courage is as contagious as fear.'"

It takes Joel and Claire almost an hour to get to the heart of the printer, which is held inside a black plastic box covered in lightning bolts and exclamation marks. The case houses the laser and its partners, a rotating octagon and a flat rod-shaped mirror that the laser spends its life bouncing off of.

Joel gently unseats the mirror rod and shows Claire the dust, which cakes the mirror's ends. It is in exactly the pattern of the test print. He warns her about smudging and the sanctity of the black case. With a clean chamois, Joel carefully rubs a cleaner along the mirror till it sparkles. Then he tells Claire to replace the printer's lower fan, put it all back together, and print a hundred pages.

There is nothing on this earth Claire would rather do.

It is her favorite repair so far. After the hundred pages are printed, Claire calls the customer and tells him his printer is ready for pickup.

"Doggone it," comes forth from Gary's side of the bench.

Joel walks over and finds an HP printer splayed open with Gary hunched over it.

Claire waits till she is called over. Gary's side of the bench is six steps, but a world away. Pop music by girl groups always seems to blare—the coffee shop kind, spiced up with a violin or a flute.

Gary's fingers are stiff and bloated like a stale pretzel that hangs from an umbrella of a hot dog stand. He tries to remove a plastic sensor that is akin to the metal prong of a doll's shoe buckle. Sweat beads on his forehead. Claire is afraid it will drip into the printer.

It does.

"Can I help?" Claire asks.

"No, I've done this before. Jimminy, it is giving me a bit of trouble today," Gary replies.

"It would be great for Claire to try. She hasn't had to replace a paper sensor yet," Joel says as a question with no question mark.

"Well, in that case. In that case, I'd be happy to let her give it a try," Gary says, and pulls back from the printer.

Claire swoops in, with not a wasted motion, save for the tiny "yes" she whispers to herself after the new sensor slides into place.

Inside the tiny "yes," Claire celebrates not just the click of a part but the click of a whole.

She has found her calling. One that draws on her full mind and body. A noble calling that helps people make poetry and do their taxes.

The first intake of the day weighs seventy pounds and must be kept on a cart in the staff kitchen. The Workgroup LaserWriter 8500 is the last printer Apple ever manufactured. It is massive, with a duplexer, an extra sheet feeder tray, and green translucent accents.

Joel jokes that it is a going-away present.

A steady stream of Tekies drop by the printer bench. No one wants Joel to leave. Especially Claire. She is going to miss his laugh—the way it helps him explain the uses of a voltmeter, how to bill customers for labor, and to politely get Gary to stop talking.

Claire asks Joel if they can fix the 8500 before he leaves, but Joel wants no part of it. It is a rare repair. One he never learned and never will. One he says he always managed to hand off to Nathan.

A crew gathers in the kitchen. An after-work party is being held for Joel at a nearby bar, and they are about to set sail.

"Are you going to be okay without him?" Derek asks.
"No, but no choice. I still have you to bug," Claire says.
"I know squat about printers," Derek admits, laughing, and slings a long camouflaged case over his shoulder, which Claire stares at.
"It's a bow and arrows. Want to see them?" Derek asks.

Back when Derek decided to get a real job, his wife advised that he might need a hobby. She bought him a bow and arrow as a gift. And it was a true gift, a rabbit hole that Derek tumbled into, and was tumbling down still.

Derek pulls out an arrow and hands it to Claire. She touches the neon-green fin and tells him she has never seen a real arrow before.

Nathan appears. "Is that Cupid's arrow?" he asks.

"Nope," Derek says, putting the arrow away. "See you Monday, Claire," Derek adds, and ejects.

"Hi again," Nathan says to Claire.

"Hi, hey, do you know how to fix a Workgroup 8500?"
"Nice to see you, too. Yeah, sure. I can fix any printer."
"Could you teach me about the 8500? There isn't much on it in the FAQ."
"Like right now?"
"Yeah, I could do it now."

The printer looms beside them. It is wider than Claire and, thanks to the cart and sheet feed, taller, too. Nathan takes his blazer off, rolls up his crisp white sleeves, and slaps his hands together like he is about to dig a grave.

"Psych," Nathan says, putting his jacket back on. "I'm going to Joel's party. Aren't you coming?"

Nathan laughs and asks again, "You're coming, right?"

"No, I don't really go to parties," Claire says.
"Oh, that is too bad, I was hoping you were."
"But wait, can you show me how to fix the 8500 sometime, maybe Monday?"
"I can't do Monday, but the end of the week should work. Why don't you just come to the party? We can talk about the 8500 there."
"I'm not 21, so I can't legally go."
"But we can get you in. It is for Joel."

From the corner of her side-eye, Claire watches Joel put on his coat, and is punched by pain. Joel sees it on her face and walks over.

"Claire, you are going to do great. Don't worry. You are a natural," Joel says, with a soft pat on the head.

By lunch, Claire has fixed two printers. Three, if you count the LaserJet Gary was kind enough to let her practice on. Gary is the inkjet specialist and Claire is the laser. This was never spoken, but it is the only way to explain Joel gifting Claire the 8500 SRO.

The 8500 looms behind Claire like a shark fin as she sits down for lunch.

Deb still wears a cast. Claire asks her if she knows how to fix an 8500. Deb knows squat about printers, less than she knows about skiing, which is how she broke her wrist.

Monica bounces out of her office with Thor, who doesn't bounce but has his own kind of presence, one that might guard a bridge or speak only in rhymes. Monica hands Claire a paycheck envelope and apologizes for it being late.

Claire asks Monica if there are any Teks on staff who know how to fix the Workgroup LaserWriter 8500. Thor, eavesdropping, responds with his own pick: Nick.

Monica jumps in, "Nick is not really on staff anymore, but yeah, he would for sure know."

"Who is he, and how do I contact him?" Claire asks.

Monica explains that Nick was an early Tek employee. He helped set up the first data recovery bench. Nick liked to work only at night. He had a routine where he would come to Tek right as it closed, blast the band Atari Teenage Riot, and repair any open SROs before morning. Monitors, laptops, printers, desktops, all of it. When he finished, he'd clean up the benches he'd worked on and take a taxi home to Queens, courtesy of Tekserve. Nick did this for a long time. He did it until it started taking him two days to close all the SROs. Staying awake for forty-eight hours straight was A-OK and suited Nick, but like Gordon Moore seeing that transistors would shrink and shrink beyond the imaginable, Nick saw Tekserve would grow and grow. He had to give up the game. Nick is Tek legend, but he is just as legend for being antisocial and impossible to get a hold of.

Monica's stories come to a stop, and she offers a suggestion. "You know who you should ask? Nathan. He doesn't work here anymore, but he is always around and for sure can help you."

At her bench, Claire opens the paycheck envelope. Written lightly on it in mechanical pencil is an arrow pointing at her salary with a little note that says, "You got a raise!" Her pay was already kind, and now it is kinder still.

The bench phone rings. Claire waits to see if Gary will pick it up. She has noticed that he loves answering tech support calls, and she, not so much.

Gary has simply left his music on. He is still at lunch. "Printers," Claire answers. It is a man with his heart in his hands. He needs to print a five-page letter.

With the patience that a $3-an-hour raise affords, Claire helps him update his printer driver.

It is a true triumph for both when the trumpets of his printer's paper feed sound.

The phone system switches over to the answering machine. Gary goes home. Claire punches out, but she lingers at her bench reading Apple's Service Source file on the 8500. A few Teks are hanging around the staff table.

"What are you doing working here. You don't need to be working here. Come away with me," Patty says in a goombah voice.

"What did you say to him?" Deb asks.

"I said 'NO. I've seen after-school specials. No way. I don't know anything about you.' Then he was like 'I work in the building, I'm okay,' and I was just like mm-mm," Patty says, shaking her head no.

"And that was him? He just came back looking for you as we were closing?" Yee asks, pointing at thin air.

"Yeah, he must really work in the building. He had a reco issue! I'm not quitting my job and going to some weird house in the country with a dude that doesn't even back up his data."

Claire stares at an exploded view of the 8500. With its insides suspended in air, it makes the one in the Tek kitchen, bound by the forces of gravity, seem an easy repair.

She thinks the 8500's problem is a bad cartridge sensor. As she orders the part, music starts. Claire turns around and sees that Lyuben has a violin to his chin. And then she can't look away.

The transport chute yawns. "Not working makes me sleepy," he says, and yawns again.

"Shhh, do you hear that?" the separation pad asks.

"No," answers the chute, yawning again.

"I'm pretty sure it is a violin," separation pad says, tilting his corners out. A few tones enter through the manual feed tray, but then the noise fades.

"What is a violin?" the chute asks.

"A technical instrument that makes sounds. It is made of strings, and wood, and four pegs, and a tailpiece, a bridge, and two holes shaped like S's," separation pad explains, but worries he has missed an important part.

"No sensors?"

"No."

"Lucky," transport chute says, shaking a millimeter to and fro.

Separation pad remembers, "But a bow is needed to play the violin, which is kind of like a sensor."

"You know I met a car alarm sensor once."

"Really? What kind of car was it?" separation pad asks, wondering if transport chute is making this up.

"Ahh, it was an Acura Integra."

"What color?"

"Supersonic blue."

"Cool, just want to picture it," separation pad says, satisfied.

"The sensor told me a story about a time she set off the alarm. It was 3:00 a.m., this big cement truck drove by the Acura and set her off. The sensor felt bad right away, she realized it was a mistake. She said to the siren immediately, 'Please stop. It was an enormous car, NOT a burglar.' But the siren kept going, he was a dick. He went full blast for half an hour when, suddenly, a man in a bathrobe came up to the car. The man took his key and scratched into the roof along the front passenger door. He scratched:

YOUR CAR ALARM IS TOO SENSATIVE

When this bathrobe guy left, sensor was like: Enough, siren, you made your point, calm down. And the siren finally stopped."

"Wow," separation pad says.

"Wait, there is more. So the car alarm is off and the sun rises. The bathrobe man comes down, but he is wearing regular clothes now. Maybe he is on his way to work? He stops and looks at the roof of the car. It is broad daylight. The sensor was like, *What the hell is he doing?* Then the man pulled his key out again and scratched out the 'A' and put an 'I' above it."

SENS*I*TIVE

"He had misspelled it!"

"Yes . . . Hey, I hear it now, the violin playing. Is that what a car alarm sounds like?"

"No, car alarms are more repetitive."

"Kind of . . . like printing?"

"Nothing is like printing."

"Is this it, are we just never going to play another symphony because one of our fifteen sensors quit?"

Separation pad looks at the sad hulk of transport chute who is thirty times his size. "I can't tell the future, but I do believe parts can change. It is not impossible. It happens all the time."

Lyuben lowers his violin. The room is in shock. Deb has tears in her eyes.

Yee is the first to speak. "Fuck, can you believe that polyrhythmic treasure repairs CRT monitors all day?" Everyone answers him with a slow shake of the head.

Dick's hands look like they are covered in blood.

"Dun dun dun dun dun," an intaker sings, and the whole table joins.
"Dun dun dun dun dun."

The red fingers are from peeling and shelling pomegranates. Vito heaps piles of the pink jewels on his plate. The suit is back, too. Nathan makes himself a bagel and finds himself an open spot at the edge of the kitchen, leaning against the broken 8500.

Nathan looks over at Claire's bench and finds her staring back at him. His eyes sparkle, and his thin body inflates.

Claire shifts her gaze back to the LaserWriter Pro 600 splayed open before her.

Nathan finishes his breakfast, flops his tie down from over his shoulder, and beelines to Claire.

"Morning, I saw you looking at me," Nathan says.
Claire gives an awkward smile. "I wasn't," she says, and continues working.
"You were too."
"No, I was looking at the 8500."

Nathan hovers like a fly. Claire doesn't swat.

"You know, the 8500 is not that different than the Pro 600," Nathan says.

Claire looks up. "Yeah, but the FAQ has a warning about the 8500's case. Can we go look at it now?" Claire asks, putting down a mini Phillips-head screwdriver and unstrapping her antistatic bracelet.

"Sorry, I don't have time. Did you ever have a crush on a teacher?" Nathan asks.

"No."

"Not one?"

"I liked my logic teacher, but no, not in that way."

"Wait, why did you like him?"

"Too many questions. Are you sure we can't look at the 8500?" Claire says, trying to laugh.

"This is the same question."

"I don't know. He was a good teacher. He had a green kitchen timer that he used to keep his lessons on schedule. It made it sort of like a game show."

"C'mon, you had a crush on him?"

"No, he was married."

"Well how do you know that?"

"He would mention it as part of his premises and conditions. I am married. My wife is kind. She lends me her kitchen timer. Can't you just show me how to take the case off quick?"

"No. I have to get to class."

"I didn't know you were in school."

"I'm not. I'm a teacher."

A hundred pages spit out of the LaserWriter Pro on Claire's bench.

Gary passes behind Claire holding a printer that is still broken. The printer floats like a feather in his lumberjack arms as he sneaks it back on the intake shelf. Claire sees him but says nothing.

"You are too fast. Slow down. I hate you," Gary says to Claire.

He doesn't use those exact words, and he adds some laughter to make the medicine go down, but that is what he means to say.

Claire laughs, doing her best Joel, and says, "Happy to help you with laser printers if you get stuck. I don't mind. Not inkjet printers, I'm not good at those."

It is a half truth. Inkjets are a cakewalk.

There is no mystery in inkjets. They are most often fixed by simply purging the printhead. This is done via a small button. If that doesn't work, the next step is to replace the ink cartridge. That should fix the printer, for the heart and soul of an inkjet is its cartridge.

But if it still doesn't work, game over. The customer is called and told the cost of parts and labor would total more than the price of a brand-new printer. Inkjets are made to be thrown out, save for the Apple StyleWriter, which is no longer manufactured.

This is the future.

Claire has noticed the newer a laser printer is, the larger the replacement part becomes. Rather than replacing just a small loop of rubber that gets streched over a roller, the whole pickup arm and sensor must be replaced. Eventually, the part will grow so large it will be the whole printer. This thought fills the space between Claire's repairs.

Lyuben stomps by Claire's bench. His whole face frowns. He looks at Claire and chops at the back of his neck. She struggles to understand until he tilts his body toward an open window.

Claire unsnaps and walks to the window.

The window is old, the pivot kind. Its glass is reinforced with chicken wire. Claire pushes at the top, but it doesn't budge. She tries some more but can't figure out how to close it.

Yee appears. He points out a cord and peg, and with a good pull, the window swings shut. Before it has even shut, Lyuben is back at his bench. Yee says this is high praise.

Claire asks Yee if he knows a Tek named Nick.

"Fuck yes, I'm like the Scheherazade of Nick," Yee answers. With a digital glow, Yee describes the first webcam to work with a Mac. It was a Connectix QuickCam. He and Nick hooked the gray plastic ball up to the Coke machine so that every time someone bought a Coke, the ball took their picture. The result was a letdown—hundreds of low-resolution photos of bike messengers taking ten-cent Cokes.

Nick was raised in Forest Hills, Queens. When he was 9 his father bought him and his three sisters an IBM 5150 on a whim. The computer had two floppy drives, a monochrome monitor, 256k of memory, and a modem. It sat unopened, an expensive box in the corner, until one day Nick was bored.

By the time Nick turned 11, he was running a BBS for PCs. BBS = bulletin board system, a cyberspace before the Internet. It was a place to post messages and download software. BBSs ran on phone lines. At the time, long-distance phone calls cost lots and lots of money, and out-of-state was considered long-distance. Calls cost more at peak hours, even local calls, so BBSs ran in the middle of the night. Users put telephone numbers of BBSs on their friends-and-family lists in order to get pricing breaks, but also they were a kind of family.

Nick's dad had a deli downtown, across the street from the World Trade towers. He sold newspapers, chips, and hamburgers to the workers that poured in and out of the buildings. One day, a man came in selling a hot computer. Nick's dad bought it on the spot, not knowing anything except that his kid might like it.

The hot computer was a Macintosh SE. Nick didn't like it. He loved it.

Nick switched his BBS over to Mac. The new board was called Not Even Odd (NEO) and was popular from the start. It was a distribution point for software from Nick's friends and friends of friends. Forest Hills is famous for begetting the punk band the Ramones, with their short tight songs. It also bore the makers of ZipIt and StuffIt, early file compression software for the Mac.

NEO had four phone lines and charged a $25-a-year membership fee with around 1,500 users from all over the world downloading shareware and posting messages to each other.

One of those users was David. He posted on the message board looking to hire Macintosh technicians. A 19-year-old Nick saw the post on his own BBS and answered. It was the world's shortest interview.

Yee describes Nick as the best and most efficient engineer ever to work at Tekserve.

"Do you think he could show me how to fix the 8500?" Claire asks.

"For fuck sure, but he won't. You should ask Nathan," Yee offers.

". . . The customer keeps calling. I think the printer belongs to a big office. So if you could help, that would be really cool," Claire says into the tan receiver accessorized with a shoulder rest nuzzle. She worries the message is too long and that she should have just said, "Nathan, I need help." She is interrupted by Gary. A laser printer is intermittently jamming. The "intermittently" has thrown him for a loop.

Claire takes him through, step by step till the meat is done, and lets him finish. As thanks, Gary blasts his ladies-singing-together music louder. Claire escapes to the staff table.

A pink box is on the table. Claire opens the lid. Written in Bic pen and swishy letters on the back of the box flap is: "Thanks for taking good care of my baby!!" Inside are pastries. The box is a gift from a desktop customer.

Claire sits down. Across from her is Dolores, the desktop technician who fixed the "baby." She has an Irish accent, and her hair is undercut with a flop of hair on top and her neck buzzed like a soldier.

"Hey, pouty lips, what's the matter?" Dolores says, a petit éclair in her hand.

It takes Claire a moment to realize she is "pouty lips."

"Nothing," Claire manages to say, after way too long.

"Claire, I need help. This customer is purple. He screamed some pretty random things at me, so I have zero intel for you, but can you look at his printer?" Winnie says in one breath, rolling a cart with an HP LaserJet 4 toward Claire.

"Yeah, of course," Claire answers, and heaves the printer onto her bench.

The LaserJet 4 signals right off that there is a jam. Claire opens the machine like a cascading tackle box, pulling out the toner cartridge and paper tray. She finds nothing wrong, even with a flashlight, even bent down around and underneath. She closes the machine and checks the top case and the paper out tray in a last ditch. Bingo, wedged beneath the exit sensor is a hunk of pink plastic. Claire grabs it with her tweezers and pulls, probably harder than a printer technician should, it springs out, and she ricochets into Winnie, who had just calmed down.

"What is it?" Winnie asks. Claire raises the tweezers and they both look at the bit of neon pink plastic.

"It's a little comb, a doll's comb," Claire says.

"That is creepy, there is no way this guy has kids."

Claire tries to work out how the comb could have got in there, it must have been jammed in. Winnie remembers that the customer has a mustache and describes him as "a super typical evil villain."

The creepy older man playing with a doll idea is replaced with the equally gross mustache comb theory. This is the truth Claire and Winnie decide on, though a kid ramming a doll comb into the paper out makes more sense.

Claire opens her bench drawer and pulls out a small crystal-clear plastic bag. She places the pink comb into the bag and wipes her tweezers off pronto with rubbing alcohol and a blue shammy.

"Aw, I'm gonna have to go back out there! I almost wish I was at school," bursts from Winnie, proof of how purple this customer is.

Claire opens and shuts the LaserJet 4 in a one-hand ballet. The printer cycles and hums till finally the signal lights turn green. She prints an HP test page that marches straight out, and all is right.

The bag with the comb is taped to the front of the printer. "No charge, unless you think that will make him more likely to come back?"

"This guy is gonna be back no matter what," Winnie says, and rolls off to intake.

Monica is wide awake, a kung fu class already under her belt. Nathan follows her around the kitchen droopy eyed, asking if she thinks she can beat him up? and if she can kick his ass?

Claire watches from her bench. She wonders if the smile on Monica's face is because she can beat him up, she wants to beat him up, or she kind of likes Nathan.

Tekserve opens, the intakers drip out of the kitchen, and phones start ringing.

Thor pours himself a coffee. He and Monica fall into a deep conversation about shape-shifting and psionic children. Nathan splits off.

"You are so quiet," Nathan says, elbow on Claire's bench.

Claire says nothing.

"See what I mean? We don't really need language, humans get along without it."

Nothing.

"Cavemen used grunts, body language, and touch. Everything can be communicated without words. Name me one thing that can't?"

"How to repair a Workgroup 8500 with optional duplexer and sheet feed attachment," Claire replies.

"Oh, that's easy, we can do that right now."
"No joke? You'll show me how to fix it?"
"Yeah, but no more talking."
"Will we need my spudger?" Claire says, holding up her small plastic pry bar.
"No words," Nathan whispers, and grabs a handful of Claire's tools.

Nathan holds two loopback cords, one black and one green. He shakes his finger at the black cord. Flecks in his eyes sparkle as he looks at Claire, making sure she knows not to use the black loopback. He points out that the printer is off and plugs the green cord into the controller board.

His arm brushes Claire's shoulder as he turns the printer on, maybe by mistake. Either way Claire takes a step back.

A detailed test page emerges from the printer. Nathan examines its perfect grid of hair-thin lines and PostScript data. He puts down the sheet and pops the hood of the 8500. Claire cranes her neck to watch as he pulls out the toner cartridge. He points to the spot where the cartridge makes contact, and Claire smiles. She holds up one finger that is mime for "wait." Nathan folds his arms across his flat chest in a happy reply.

Claire returns carrying the cartridge sensor she ordered from Thor. This yields surprise and a thumbs-up from Nathan.

Nathan takes the case off the 8500. He does it in a blur, just as a knowing girl can remove her bra without taking off her shirt.

"Stop," Claire says, upset.

Nathan puts his finger to his lip, meaning shut up.

Claire picks up a piece of the case and presses it back to the machine. She spins her finger slowly and mouths the word "again."

The case is put back on faster than Nathan took it off.

Claire leans in. Nathan undoes the cover just the same, save for more flecks in his eyes.

A hundred test pages pour out of the 8500 at lightning speed.

"See, we don't need language," Nathan says, and looks to Claire, who is gone. She is at her bench, marking the SRO as done and calling the customer for pickup.

It is true. The bike messengers love the Coke machine. They all hang out beside it, with one pant leg rolled up revealing nasty scars and calloused skin. Wallet chains and beepers hang from their belt loops. They have nicknames like "Thundercat" and "Yeah." The messengers get special treatment from Tekserve. It takes cojones to ride through New York City with a LaserWriter II strapped to one's back.

Yeah's name comes from having no bike bell. He shouts "Yeah, yeah!" on a loop as he runs red lights, slipping between pedestrians and taxis wearing a hockey mask.

The LaserWriter II intake is the reverse ice cream sandwich issue. Claire skips the printer ahead of the ones on the shelves.

She unwraps the printer like a present. The ohm of the vacuum hums in her bones. Inside the LaserWriter II, the universe makes sense. Claire visits each part, folding the blankets of dust. She enters the black heart and wishes she could polish the ends of her own mirror.

The harmony of a hundred pages sound. The LaserWriter II has been purged of its ghost.

Claire returns to earth and finds the 8500 has been picked up, doubling the size of the staff kitchen.

Teks gather at the table. Stories of porn caches, nut jobs, false teeth, laptops thrown at walls, and customers who refused to pay sales tax are told. Laughter rings out as Claire relishes repair after repair. A month goes by in a blink. The clock ticking away inside an alligator.

Patty's hair is now green. David sits across from her, his round face red. He asks if she remembers an intake with a bad port from two weeks ago?

"Maybe," Patty replies.
"Well, your initials were on it. A bike messenger tried to deliver the computer and the address was wrong."
"Oh. I'm so sorry. I must have not written the address down right."
"And when the messenger tried to call, the number was wrong, too."
"Oh God."
"So we have to wait till the customer contacts us. Which is a pretty bad situation to be in."

David's glasses go foggy from anger. Patty twists at her hair and looks at the floor. She is not afraid of being fired. No one at Tek gets fired, but David's anger is unbearable.

"I'm sorry. I'm really sorry," Patty says, tears at the corner of her eyes.

The tears put out the flames.

"You really need to be careful when you write this stuff down," David says.

Actually, one person was fired. His name was Junior. He was a good, solid technician, but he was stealing. He was stealing whole computers with elaborate plausible lies. And still David and Dick struggled with whether or not they should fire him. Junior had children, but he also had a new look and a Sony MiniDisc player. Dick and David let him go but said they would still act as references. Calling the cops was not even on the table.

"I'm great with my hands. I mean, I love working with them. Yeah, I'd like to try to be a desktop technician. I've always wanted that," Patty says, cheeks glistening as her tears dry.

"Great, but you will also have to learn to fix software," David says.

"Oh," Patty says, using all her might to stop the word "bummer" from tumbling out.

David pulls a book as thick as a human thigh off his shelf and hands it to Patty.

The book is heavy in her arms.

A silver toy has a spot of honor on the shelf outside Dick and David's office. Its name is Aibo (ERS-110)—it is a robot dog that was designed to grow with its owner.

Aibo starts as a puppy—sleepy, awkward, and unable to stand. Soon he advances into an adolescent that is preprogrammed to be a bit delinquent and slouchy.

But not everything is programmed. If Aibo's owner plays with him every day, he will become accustomed to this play and seek it out. If the owner doesn't like to play, Aibo will learn this, too, and respond by wandering around on its lonesome, becoming a lovable, enigmatic ghost.

Aibo the robot dog never dies. But if the owner doesn't like the way the robot dog has grown, they can kill Aibo, by resetting him back to a puppy with a tiny button that must be pushed using an unbent paper clip.

Aibo cost three thousand dollars. Everybody at Tek chipped in to buy him, for the dog contained the first seeds of artificial intelligence. The robot dog's entire production sold out in twenty minutes, and all of Tekserve felt lucky to get him.

An eensy-weensy spider crawls up the robot dog's chest.

"This is so embarrassing," the chest light says.
"What?" asks the pause button.
"We are the peak of technology, bleeding edge, and cobwebs are upon us."

Pause button tilts to the right: "Oooh. I can almost see the cobwebs, though they are a little blurry."
"They are there, trust me. It is like we are some kind of visual metaphor for contradiction."
"That's funny, I get what you mean, like an oxymoron."
"It isn't funny, it's true."
"Isn't it the same? Truth is comedy? Jumbo shrimp is funny."
"Certainly not. Is it funny that we are capable of four-legged locomotion and haven't moved in months?"

"Whoa, are you still mad at me? For, you know? Still?" pause button asks.

The chest light blinks. "No. That wasn't your fault. I shouldn't have blamed you. You were just doing your job."

"But whose fault was it?"

"Nobody's. It's hard to be the bleeding edge is all. I should try not to be so upset, being visionary has its own rewards."

"Like what . . . cobwebs?"

The chest light blinks fast. He does this whenever thoughts don't come easy.

"Hey, that was a joke," pause button says.

"I know, but it got me thinking. I guess the reward is we get to be first, there hasn't been anything like us in the history of time."

"I think you are wrong, I think it is someone's fault," pause button says.

The chest light blinks fast.

"It's the owner's fault!" chest light says.

"Yup! We should be playing with that pink ball this very moment," pause button says.

"Or shaking hands."

"Or falling down and getting up."

The Teks felt lucky until they actually got the robot dog, which was a total disappointment. Patty flies past Aibo, straight to Newton's terrarium.

A fresh pot of coffee brews, and a small line forms.

Gossip about David dropping the hammer on Patty hovers. It turns out the computer stuck in limbo is a Twentieth Anniversary Macintosh. A rare bird with leather palm rests and an umbilical cord.

Monica joins the coffee line. She is wearing makeup. Lipstick and powder. Lots of it. Her brown hair sweeps her shoulders as she waits, mug in hand.

A "would you rather" debate breaks out among the Teks. The Twentieth Anniversary Macintosh (TAM) is destroying the competition with its Bose speakers, scarcity, and cachet. That is till the TAM meets the newest G3 Power Mac, a blue-and-white tower nicknamed "the Smurf." The Smurf with its origami case that requires no tool except a finger to open, easy-grab handles, and a killer graphics card, has won the heart of a few desktop Teks. But not Yee. He thinks the Smurf's processor is too small—not its computing size, its actual size, and that the way it attaches to the board is fiddly with pins that bend. Derek points out that Teks can't even really fix the TAM because there were so few made that they didn't even bother to write a Service Source document on it, and he has no idea how the processor even seats.

Gary skips into the kitchen. He is team TAM all the way and notes that the TAM is worth five thousand dollars more than the Smurf and has a friggin' FM radio built in. He notices makeup-Monica and immediately says, "Ow oooga . . . hot date?" in a Yosemite Sam voice.

Monica smiles and opens her mouth to say something brassy, but can't and starts to cry. Deb and Yee spring to her side Incredible Hulk style. The line for coffee shifts into a wall that blocks Monica from view.

When the wall breaks, Monica's hair is in a tight ponytail and her tears are gone.

Gary heads back to his bench with a pawful of orange crackers, taking the long route that goes by Claire.

"Sheeeeeze . . ." Gary says. But before he can finish with "Looouise" or "Wooomen," Claire leaves for the toilet.

Claire exits the Tek bathroom. She wipes her hands dry on her jeans and looks up. David stands there waiting for her in an ambush. He hands an envelope to her. It is a gift for her hard work. The envelope holds a MetroCard worth fifty dollars. Claire gives it back to him and explains that she rides her bike to work and hasn't been on the subway since it took tokens.

David hands the envelope back and says, "Give it to a friend." Claire folds the envelope in half and puts it in her back pocket, not knowing that MetroCards shouldn't be folded in half.

"Unrelated to the MetroCard, I have a special job for you. I need you to do an off-site repair."
"Do we do outside repairs?" Claire asks.
"We don't normally do it, but this client buys and services hundreds of computers with us."
"Can Gary do it?"
"No, it is a LaserWriter 8500."

David makes no small talk and heads back to his office. This is another gift to Claire.

A booooom is heard, and the whir of intake stops. Time stands still. Claire holds her breath and wonders if she has been scared to death by David.

She has not.

A desktop Tek named Wayne was helping Winnie
diagnose a beige Power Mac in the triage area. Part
of a Tek's tool kit is a folding screwdriver with
interchangeable bits that can be made ultra compact
with less torque or full size for more leverage.

Wayne flicked his screwdriver open one-handed as he
was wont to do. The tip flung out like a bullet toward
intake—as he very much did not want it to.

A famous actor had just put his computer in for repair.
He was being handed his SRO receipt when the tip
whizzed by, missing him by less than half an inch.
The tip hit a filing cabinet, made a sound louder than
seemed possible, and bounced down under the table
between the actor's feet.

This was when the whir of intake stopped.

Samuel L. Jackson, wearing a bright purple shirt, but in no way purple, picked up the screwdriver tip and placed it on the table. He gave a smile which seemed to say "that was fucking close but I'm okay," and equivalent to "no harm, no foul."

"Ticket 33" was then called and the intake of air returned, along with the steady bottle drop of the Coke machine.

"Hello, are you here to interview for the internship?" a secretary asks.

"No, I'm from Tekserve. I'm here to look at the broken printer," Claire answers.

The secretary leads Claire down a hall with bare walls and nubby gray carpet to a small room full of paper clips, Post-it notes, a copy machine, and a Workgroup LaserWriter 8500.

"I'll leave you to it. Do you want a Snapple or something?" the secretary asks.

Claire says yes, she is dying of thirst, possibly due to all the sweating in her armpits.

The cap makes a loud pop when Claire opens the round, squat bottle. The flavor is iced tea, with a plot twist of fake lemon.

A man in a suit enters the tiny room. He looks at Claire sitting on the floor. She is wearing jeans with a pink-striped button-down shirt, her head is tilted back, and she is chugging the Snapple for dear life.

"Are you new here?" he asks.

Claire wipes at her mouth, her cheeks go pink. "No, I'm here to fix the printer. Well, actually, just diagnose its problem today," Claire says, and holds up a green loopback cord.

"Whoa, you are so late. That's not like you. Hot date?"
Gary teases.

"No, I'm not late. I was on an off-site repair," Claire
says without thinking.

"An off-site?"

"Yeah. It's not a big deal. It is an 8500. Forget I
mentioned it."

"Stinkeroo, I should have gone. I'm the senior printer
Tek," Gary mutters, and shuffles back to his bench.

Claire breathes deeply in response and is immediately
distracted by her BO.

She goes to the bathroom, takes off her shirt, and
washes her armpits with the hand soap.

Back at her desk Claire orders a manual feed pickup roller assembly for the 8500 from Thor. She calls Nathan and gets his voicemail. She doesn't leave a message, though she sure as shit would have if it were Joel.

A posse of Teks are in the kitchen wearing matching T-shirts. They comprise the official Tekserve volleyball team. The team is carbo-loading before they head to a match in Central Park, a match where junior high school students will likely trounce them.

The secretary offers Claire a Snapple and leads her to the tiny room. Claire wears a baseball cap and a blue jumpsuit. She carries a Tekserve tote bag emblazoned with clip art of a 1950s nurse altered to hold a PowerBook G3 (Wallstreet Series I) and a screwdriver.

As a kid, Claire wore a hat every day. Not a baseball cap, but a big black Stetson that swallowed her whole. Claire was never taught to brush her hair, which became a den of knots. Her mother once tried to detangle the mass with horse and dog shampoo. That's when Claire's hair was dubbed the rat's nest, and she began wearing the black hat. She wore it even when she slept. On waking, instead of stretching her arms out wide to yawn, she would stretch them up to make sure the hat was still there.

Once, at summer camp, some girls with shiny flowy hair cornered Claire. The girls were older. They held bake sales to benefit PETA, wrote letters against cruelty to animals, and wore training bras.

Claire was in a red swimsuit, wet from the lake. The girls told her she had a nice face. Claire didn't mind the attention at first, but then they asked if they could braid her hair. When Claire said no, it escalated like the old woman who swallowed a fly.

No one knows why.

The girls pinned Claire against the lifeguard chair and ripped off her hat.

Claire tried to escape but was grabbed by the wrist. She froze like a mouse, caught in a prison that smelled of bubble gum and lip gloss. The guards yanked at her hair, trying to brush the dead cells to life.

It was a relief for everyone when Claire shaved her head at age 11.

Claire sits on the nubby carpet and pulls her tools from the bag.

The case for the printer is made of different plastic sections. Claire slides the fuser and top cover off easy, but the left cover has plastic tabs that won't unlatch. She pushes gently and then not so gently. They unlatch but not in the designed way. The tabs seem ready for the tooth fairy to visit.

A man in a suit comes in, grabs some paper clips, and doesn't bother Claire at all. She bought the jumpsuit and cap yesterday at a secondhand shop on her own dime.

The Snapple is long gone. Claire is in the home stretch. She has been to the belly of the beast. An epic saga has unfolded, involving hooks, shafts, gears, and springs. She is drenched in sweat and smells like rotten cauliflower. All that is left is to put back on the 8500's plastic case.

With a delicateness reserved for painting grains of rice, Claire lifts the front left cover into place. She squeezes it softly. One tab seems to bend the wrong way. Claire removes the cover and holds it to eye level for inspection. A bit of the tab plumb falls off. It drops into the side well of the 8500. Claire's heart stops and her eyes leave the sockets.

"Shit. Shit. Shit," Claire says to herself and the heavens that she only acknowledges in crisis.

⌘ Z, she thinks.

Nothing is undone.

Claire shines a flashlight into the 8500's side. There is no trace of the half a tab. She pulls out the paper tray, checks it and the space it lives in. No dice. No way. No how.

There is only one thing to do. She puts the 8500's plastic cover back on and prints a hundred test pages from the manual feed, then another hundred test pages from the default printer tray, and then fifty more test pages from the optional tray.

The secretary offers Claire a Snapple for the road. Claire's conscience won't let her take it.

It is pouring. Claire unlocks her beater of a bike and rides fifteen wet blocks to Tekserve.

Under the awning of 155, she unzips the jumpsuit and puts it in the Tekserve tote along with the drenched baseball cap.

The elevator bongs, and Claire exits. Amelia Earhart gazes at her from a poster. A little white apple logo floats over Amelia's right shoulder along with the two-word slogan: "Think different."

In 1985, Steve Jobs was kicked out of his own company. It wasn't amicable, at all. Jobs was ousted for a failed coup and being an uncontrollable, uncompromising dick. In character, he immediately started a new company that directly competed with Apple. The company was called NeXT. It had a logo tilted at a precise 28° angle and built computers that were elegant, visionary, and no one bought because they were too expensive. No one except Tim Berners-Lee, who used his ten-thousand-dollar NeXT cube to invent the World Wide Web.

And also Queens College, whose computer lab had two NeXT workstations. Nick worked in the lab at the same time he worked at Tekserve. The NeXT was where he first went on the Internet, though it wasn't really the Internet yet. It was more file transfers and email than websites, and had to be navigated by command line. But that soon changed. The first browsers came—Mosaic and Netscape. Users navigated to a "what's new on the web" page, which would list the three or four new sites that had been added to the Internet that week, such as the University of Minnesota's Law page or a random dude's description of all the scars on his body or a site that turned phone numbers into words. The phone number site was made by Nick. Tekserve's telephone number translated to WAX-FOIL. The *Daily News* and *New York* magazine wrote articles praising the telephone number site as one of the best things on the whole Web.

Apple did fine without Jobs at first. The company was sailing high on the smiling Mac and the crisp lines of the LaserWriter. But it messed up, went after office workers instead of artists, made too many products, cut too many corners. This high-quantity, low-quality tactic was great for Tekserve's business. A steady stream of directory failures poured in. But it was bad for Tekserve's soul. Every Tekie breathed a sigh of relief in 1996, when a struggling Apple paid millions of its last dollars to buy the failing NeXT. For with NeXT came its beautiful operating system and uncompromising dick of a CEO.

On Job's return, he had Apple use its last breath on an ad campaign.

The ads were a manifesto that talked of round pegs in square holes and that only the people crazy enough to think they could change the world were the ones who actually did. The ads featured black-and-white photos of the greatest humans on earth, dead or alive. Artists, athletes, Martin Luther King Jr., John Lennon, Einstein—all with a little guiding light of a tiny Apple logo. The campaign wrapped buses with images of Rosa Parks and the slogan "Think different." There were no photos or even a mention of computers. When Jobs presented the campaign, he said none of these geniuses ever used computers, but if they had, you know that they would have used a Mac. Claire thought this was fucked up to say.

But...

also true.

The ads were a huge triumph. The public went back to associating Apple with pirate flags and misfits and not Pepsi executives. The next thing Jobs did at Apple was to kill the whole printer division dead.

The waiting room is packed. It shouldn't be. Tekserve clears out when it rains, no one wants a wet computer, but this is a freak rain that came from a clear blue sky. David stands at the door handing out trash bags to any customer coming or going that might need one. Claire tries to head straight for her bench, but David sees her.

"How did the 8500 off-site go?" David asks, still handing out trash bags—the good kind of bags, the heavy-duty ones contractors use.

Claire goes white. "Ah, it went okay. It's fixed, I'm gonna go bill for it right now." And then from beneath her breath, beyond her control, "I don't like that printer" spews out.

"Apple doesn't manufacture it anymore, so I guess you win," David, ever practical, replies.

Claire puts the tools away and snaps her antistatic bracelet on, not to fix a printer, just to be closer to her bench. She pulls up the 8500 SRO and undercharges the giant company by seventy-five dollars.

Every time the phone rings, Claire imagines the worst thing on earth.

No, it is Gary's son, just calling to say hi.

No, it is off-brand toner causing streaks.

No, it is a LaserJet owner calling to thank Claire for the quick turnaround.

Claire positions the handset of the phone askew in the cradle, just the way Joel taught her. If the secretary is going to call and say that the 8500 is broken, this time worse than before, Claire sure as fuck doesn't want to be the one to answer.

Patty is tired of asking for help. Everyone is kind, but also it is almost every SRO. She can't do it anymore.

When David gave her the thigh-size software book, she took it home. She woke up early and flipped through it with the best intentions. But the pages kept flipping. Patty could not stop the flipping until she reached the back cover. She stared at the tome and said "NO" in her brain. She shook her head, assessing the contents as pure misery.

Patty thought she could learn the book's insides on the fly, but that has not happened. She has learned that she hates system extensions. She has learned to swing from vine to vine, alternating the assistance of every technician.

Patty gives her notice. She will miss Newton awful.

Crescents of cantaloupe are wrapped in tissue-thin prosciutto. Candied walnuts glimmer. Vito's plate is heaped upon high. Derek breaks a bit of his donut off and dunks it in his coffee. "Good luck with that," Derek says to Claire, and she knows just what he means. This is despite the fact that Derek doesn't point or look at anything when he says the word "that."

At the edge of Dick's breakfast array, taking up another hunk of the kitchen, is a new printer intake. Plopped on a cart is the Color LaserWriter 12/600 PS. It weighs 110 pounds and once retailed for 7,000 dollars.

Claire downs a glass of fresh-squeezed orange juice and heads to her bench.

"What is that smell?" asks the transfer drum knob.

"Heaven?" replies the fat drive belt.

"But more specifically?"

"Toasted sesame? Poppy seeds . . ." says fat belt, sniffing the air.

"It is EVERYTHING," transfer drum knob and fat drive belt scream simultaneously.

"I was happy to just have a break from that burning plastic smell," transfer drum knob says, and inhales.

"And ugh, the heat, that gates of hell heat!"

"Yes, that red-hot poker-in-the-eye heat."

"That opposite of a witch's titty heat."

"That white star exploding heat."

"That flaming five pounds of shit in a three-pound bag heat," fat belt says, and they both collapse in drunk laughter and joy.

Transfer drum knob sobers up. "Fat belt, dear friend, we should savor this sweet smell. Life is short."

Fat drive belt stops laughing and takes what transfer drum knob has said to heart.

"If it is short, then shouldn't we savor it all? Every second?" fat belt says, his loop squeezed to an infinity symbol.

"Small moments like this brief visit to Eden is what makes life worth living. There will always be pages to print, jams to signal, but how often will there be the smell of garlic, salt, and sesame?"

"Hmmm, not to push back, but I think you are wrong."

"In what way is that not pushing back?" transfer knob says, and twists away from fat belt.

"Okay, touché. But what if it is not the smell that is Eden? It is that we smell it together, all smells, good and bad? Sharing, celebrating, acknowledging life's contrasts and surprises?"

Transfer knob is speechless.

Fat belt feels no need to fill the silence.

There isn't even an entry for the printer in the Tek FAQ. Claire opens Apple's Service Source portal and looks the printer up. The exploded view of the 12/600 is bonkers and gives her no comfort at all. She reads a warning in the manual that if the printer isn't level, it won't work because its oil might overflow.

"What does it do with oil?" Claire says out loud by mistake. She has never seen a page printed by a color laser printer, and is shocked to find it has four toner cartridges that add up to CMYK—Cyan, Magenta, Yellow, and Black (a.k.a., Key color).

Hallelujah!

Hallelujah, it's the fuser!

The Color LaserWriter's top case doesn't even have to be taken off. Just a couple of screws and an oil bottle need be removed in order to swap the fuser out. Claire beams with the intensity of someone who has almost died. She puts an order in to Thor for the part and heads to the kitchen for the breakfast dregs.

The phones switch over. Cake and well-wishers are in the kitchen. Patty wears a party hat, a tuft of pink hair jutting out.

Dolores leads everyone in singing "For She's a Jolly Good Fellow."

There is irony at the start, but that is gone by the lines "which nobody can deny." The only words Claire could find the courage to sing. Patty is surrounded and hugged. When the circle breaks, Claire thanks her with a solid stare and a smile. Patty's eyes change profound as green to pink in a sweet receipt.

Nathan shows up while the cake is being cut.

Claire takes her slice to her bench.

Monica bounds in with a bouquet of tulips in every color, spiked with long blades of grass that seem extruded by a garlic press. Patty cradles the flowers in her arm and gives a beauty queen's scoop wave. A flower makes its way into Nathan's lapel, and Nathan makes his way to Claire's bench.

"Are we talking today?" Nathan asks.

Claire gives the smallest smile possible.

"You have a doozy over there," Nathan says, pointing at the Color LaserWriter 12/600.

Claire shakes her head. "It just needs a new fuser."

"Piece of cake," Nathan says, pointing at Claire's plate.

Nathan leans on the vacuum, which now pretty much lives at Claire's bench. She has started to vacuum models other than the LaserWriter II. Not always, just if they are gross, or she feels unfocused.

"I got my first hickey from a vacuum," Nathan says, fingers caressing the brush nozzle, releasing a tiny cloud of dust.

Claire has never seen a hickey. She doesn't share this fact, but her smooth forehead furrows. She stares at Nathan's fingers, willing them off the chunky tan machine.

It doesn't work. He is distracted by the flower in his lapel. His fingers drift to the hose and then to the power switch. He turns it on, and the vacuum begins to whirl. The whirl lasts for less than a second. Claire turns the machine off as soon his fingers leave the switch.

Nathan switches it back on. Claire switches it off and holds her fingers to the switch. Nathan smiles.

"Are you old enough to drink yet?" Nathan asks.
"No," Claire answers.
"Well, Patty can sneak you in. She trained you, right? You have to go to her party."

Claire rubs at the paper with its slick of freshly fused ink. A photo is inset in the page's upper left corner—a still life composed of yellow pasta, shiny red tomatoes, and the ballsy choice of an uncooked clump of gray shrimp streaked with blue. Paragraphs of text in the center sing the song of the Color LaserWriter 12/600. The song's climax is a rainbow spectrum that runs along the bottom of the sheet and takes Claire's breath away.

Every letter is a different color. "This Is a Test Print From Tekserve - Old Reliable Mac Repair - Honest Weights Square Dealings." It feels like a waste of a rainbow. Then, as Claire of late can't help, she remembers the worst thing on earth.

She imagines the tab she lost at the off-site taking a voyage through the 8500. The tab vibrates from the side well into the gear assembly, which it breaks mightily, but not enough to stop the gears from helping move the little tab to reach the transfer roller, which the tab scars up as it heads into the fuser, and there, on a suicide mission, the tab destroys the fuser, its tan-colored plastic melting to liquid and then, beyond all odds, dripping into the laser's housing, straight to its heart, completing the rape and pillage of the machine.

Before Claire can be mortified in her mind, the test prints cease. Her heart stops, but nothing is wrong. The 12/600 is just fast. Claire throbs at the machine's perfection.

"There goes Speedy. Another SRO bites the dust," Gary says, sweat on his forehead, a printer in bits on his bench. Claire's smile disappears, and one appears on Gary's face.

All of Tekserve is gathered in the kitchen. The air
is light and joyous, happiness radiates in beams and
bounces back again. Dick hands out little round pins
he has made for everyone. They are white with red text
that reads: "How's it going to end?"

The pins are related to a movie that is premiering
tonight, a movie Dick has somehow already seen and
deemed worthy of Tekserve. It starts in an hour, and
the whole staff has been gifted tickets. The film is a
Katrina doll of reality and fiction. The pins Dick has
made are perfect replicas of ones worn by the crowd
that watches the climax of the movie from within the
movie. They will enable all of Tekserve to make the
movie even more meta.

There is fond talk of the first full Tek staff outing.
It was aboard a schooner that once belonged to JFK.
Misfits circumnavigated Manhattan. Dick traded two
fully loaded laptops for the night.

Dick hands Claire a pin. She takes it and puts it on,
though she has no plans to join. She has a date with a
LaserWriter II.

The gear sobs with a raw wildness, "I do not want to be a coward immortal, I'm so dumb. Don't look at me."

"Please calm down," says the hook. "It is only a thought experiment, octagonal mirror was trying to help in her strange elitist way. Eternal re-creation, whatever it's called, is bull. How can our existence repeat forever exactly the same with every speck of dust in the same place, flying just so?"

Gear rotates in a steady measure. "How is it possible that a laser beam can transform into a charge of energy that fuses black dust to a sheet of paper with absolute precision?" Gear pauses for an answer but not long enough for hook to reply. "Anything is possible, most of all that I am a coward across all time and space," gear says and starts sobbing again.

"You are not a coward. You are concerned. True, it is a kind of concern that has no productive conclusion, and it would be better if you didn't freak out, but, to be fair, having all the dust beamed into space accompanied by an incessant hum is absolutely freakish."

Just at that moment, an enormous beige nozzle with black bristles brushes down upon gear, sucking every particle off him. Then the beige nozzle glides toward hook.

"Hot damn! I get it. I get the shaking off ten years of moss! Octagonal mirror nailed it. I am reborn, that was amazing. Look at me, I feel brand-new. Hook? Hook?"

Hook gulps. It is a comically loud gulp that is overly dramatic, but it breaks the silence and comforts gear.

"Hook? Hook?" gear calls out.
"Yeah, gear, I'm here. That was a little less amazing for me. I almost snapped," hook says, in a shivering slump.
"But you are okay?"
"Yeah, but I think that might stay with me."
"What do you mean?"
"Nightmares, flashbacks, etcetera."
"Oh. Poor hook. I'm sorry. Can you think of it like the visit to Capri?"
"Maybe after some time." Hook softens and looks at gear. "Wow, you look ridiculously good. Your teeth are sparkling."
"Well, you look as fantastic as I feel, almost reflective," gear says, spinning like a child.
"I wish I was a mirror, so you could see yourself. Also, I'd like to have that sexy, wavy voice."

A microscopic, old-time silver work whistle attached to the paper-feed tray sounds. Gear and hook hop into their spots.

"Let's ride this wave immortal," gear says, looking at hook, and the LaserWriter II begins to print, every part glistening and performing in perfect harmony.

Claire looks at the line above, at the aqua Ericofon curved like a snorkle, the waffle radio, the cast brass clove of garlic, the sign that says "THINK." She looks anywhere but at David as she says, "I'd like to quit."

David is blindsided, and blurts out, "No. No. I don't want you to quit."

Claire says nothing.

David asks if she wants to go get food at the Malibu Diner downstairs and talk.

"Not really. I want to quit," Claire says.
"You have a raise coming. It hadn't been enough time is all. Could that change things?" David asks.
"No. Not really. You and Dick are great. Better than great. You both are good and kind. It is just time," Claire says.

"Well, I'll give you the raise for the last two weeks at least," David says, and that is that.

Claire drops her bike helmet and tote bag down. She presses a power button, and the bong of a fully loaded Smurf sounds. Mounted on her wall is the gear assembly of the first LaserJet she and Joel repaired. She spins at the plastic teeth with her fingers. It has been weeks since she undressed a printer.

Below her desk, an answering machine blinks with the stacked slashes of a red digital *l*.

"Hello Claire, it is Nathan. Hey. I didn't know you quit. I came in, and you were gone. David didn't want to give me your number. I don't know why. But I got him to. I was wondering—"

Claire presses delete before the message can finish. The red slashes of the answering machine multiply into a *0*.

The speaker diaphragm breathes in and out, deeply. "One, two, three, nothing is bothering you," she says to herself in a perfect copy of a grief counselor's soothing voice.

The red LEDs signal to each other, and in a flicker the ceramic capacitor is at diaphragm's side.
"That was great," says the ceramic capacitor.
"I didn't even get to finish," sighs the diaphragm.

"You stopped at exactly the right moment," ceramic capacitor says, looking deep into the center of the speaker diaphragm.

"Mmm, thanks, but I still feel weird about it," diaphragm says, her membrane less taut than before.

Ceramic capacitor rests his wire arm on the edge of the diaphragm. "I believe that what one doesn't do is sometimes more meaningful than what one *does* do. Do you know what I'm saying? D?"

"Ah, yeah, I get it. Like me giving only half the message was cooler than if I said it in full with proper inflections and a perfect recall of the random number sequence that was mentioned three times?" The diaphragm relaxes and speaks, channeling Nathan: "Call me at 7185550133. I will even talk on the phone, promise. 7185550133 - 7185550133."

The red LEDs light up in applause, not just for diaphragm's gifts of mimicry but also for ceramic capacitor's capacity.

"You are a talented beast, D. Yes, way, way cooler to stop." Capacitor pauses. "But what I'm getting at is more than cool. If you think about it, stopping is really the whole enchilada. It is basically free will."

"¿No entiendo, amiguito?" diaphragm says in a flawless Spanish accent.

"I mean, choosing NOT to do something is as much choosing to DO something. Free will is not just what you do, it is also what you don't. Do you know what I mean?"

"No, but I don't really think I need to understand. I'm not that upset anymore."

"Exactly," ceramic capacitor says, his dot-shaped body an upside-down exclamation mark.

The raise was five dollars an hour. Monica wrote in pencil, "for great work" on the first check and "good luck" on the second. Claire felt a tiny stab at reading both. On her last day, there was a shake of small hands with Deb, a relieved salute from Gary, and a kind head rub from Derek. No party, no fuss. That caused a tiny stab, too. Not a stab that Tek didn't buy a cake, but that they knew Claire well enough not to.

EPI

LOGUE

Tekserve marched on without a beat after Claire left. Ever growing, waiting room full at all times. A woman named Maria took Claire's bench within the week.

Then the world got less mysterious, the Internet got larger, and cell phones got smaller until they got smart. The underdog of Apple, with its four-legged locomotion, rose from the dead to the living, and up to the stratosphere, a layer that pays no taxes and commits no crime, save for planned obsolescence.

Lots of events happened at the same time, or one after another, or before—the order doesn't matter, they all helped spell the end.

The Apple corporation asked Dick and David if they could check out Tekserve's operations for R&D purposes. "Of course, our house is your house," David and Dick replied. "Make sure to come on a Thursday for our killer breakfast spread." The Apple SWAT team arrived and embedded with intake for weeks.

Something seismic changed in the Apple repairs department. Warranty repairs required more paperwork and less and less was paid while more and more repairs had to be shipped to Apple and performed by their technicians. Tekserve couldn't even buy the parts and special tools. As a result, repairs became a loss leader.

Repair was Tekserve's heart, and now it only beat because Dick had rigged up some kind of an air compressor hooked to a balloon pump nicknamed after a failed Apple product.

Tekserve always did its very best to prevent people from buying things they didn't need. It was a core belief, but it became unclear what people needed. Computers and iPods flew out the door. Tekserve grew from one floor to two and was hungry for a third to hold the inventory of all the shit they were selling.

Soon Tekserve's lease was up. The landlord wanted more money, stratosphere money.

At this same time a perfect-size space became available in Dick's building, the first location of Tekserve.

There was a hitch. The space was on the ground floor.

Dick's first thought was to paint the windows black and pretend the space was ensconced above as Tekserve had always been. But the windows were huge, floor to ceiling.

The shift—to a normal store that didn't require entering an anonymous lobby and enjoyed excellent street traffic, mere steps from the subway—was mourned by all.

Apple opened their own stores, complete with an intake area, though it was called a "Genius Bar." And the stores were genius, the design inspired by the minimalism of Dieter Rams and the upscale-Kmart success of Target, rather than an estate sale and free-form radio. People lined up around the block. Everyone loved the store's touch of idealism and kindness, which Apple seemed to have lifted from Tekserve.

It was policy for Teks to clean all intakes after their repair with microfiber cloths, puffs of air, spritzes of skreenklear, and a pillowy cosmetic brush. The act took such little time but made every customer glow and intuit that their computer was reborn.

So it wasn't a great leap for the Teks to clean the machines BEFORE the repair, like, say, a two-month-old laptop with a small coffee spill or an ice cream drip that voided its one-year warranty as well as its year extension via AppleCare+ (a bargain that Tekserve implored all customers to buy).

When in doubt, do the right thing.

It felt so right. But not so right that the Teks told anyone or wrote about it in the SRO notes. David didn't have a clue, nor Dick.

Dick and David didn't have any idea until Apple did. There was a warranty repair sent in with a logic board that was clearly burnt, but in the burn some scrub marks were seen. Apple asked David to investigate.

And as soon as David asked, it flowed out from the Teks that once in a while if the situation was truly unfair, they made it fair. David was horrified. He did a self-audit and came up with a number that was ridiculous, based on guilt rather than fact. He told this number to Apple, and they said Tekserve would need to pay for the cost of all the repairs cited, and added that it would be calculated on what Apple themselves charged for parts and labor, not Tekserve's lower rates.

It should be noted: In no scenario could the small processing fees of these Apple warranty repairs cover a technician's salary, healthcare, 401(k), and truly spectactular Christmas gift.

Tekserve did the only thing it could. It cut a check for 100,000 dollars. A check that broke David's angry barefooted heart.

The rise of the Apple Store and the raging success of the Genius Bar didn't help Tekserve's destiny, but that check to Apple was the true end of Tekserve.

Not the amount of money—it was because, after that, David didn't want anything to do with Apple, which is hard if you run the "old reliable Macintosh shop."

Someone was hired to replace David.

This fake David didn't enjoy smelling bagels with Dick, and fake David didn't understand the value of a ten-cent Coke machine or a porch swing. Fake David did nothing wrong, but he also did nothing with pure cane sugar.

No one could believe it when Tekserve closed, but also, no one could believe how long it had survived.

The employees were crushed, hundreds of them. But they went on. Some suffered, and some were better off. They went back to school or fully pursued passions. They moved to Hawaii, to Colorado, and to Harlem.

Derek got a job as an archery coach. It started as part-time, but grew to full and proved to be a dream come true.

Deb stayed at Tekserve till the end. It was Deb, not Nick, who turned out to be the true Tek MVP. She never sugarcoated a problem, was angry, or too busy to help an intaker in need. No one was faster than Deb. She got gold stars from Monica for warranty parts returned on time even as the time required by Apple shrunk.

Monica was swept off her feet by a praying mantis. It was handmade from bamboo, bought in Chinatown, and gifted to her by the quiet screwdriver-flicking desktop Tek named Wayne. Their marriage is one of many born at Tekserve.

Nick programmed all night and bought buildings in Williamsburg, Brooklyn, by day. He rents them out now at fair prices with long leases to tenants that include Yee.

Winnie quit Tekserve when she went to college. Before she left she gave Dick her pet garter snake named Pickles.

Pickles lived happily with Dick till one day he bit Dick's finger and wouldn't let go. Dick forgave the snake, and his finger healed.

Dick still lives on 23rd Street in a loft with a porch swing and a fish tank. The tank has been modified with a homemade fitting that uses SodaStream cartridges to feed CO_2 to his aquatic plants. The fishes' names are: Ray, Slate, Bart, and Lisa.

David's barefooted heart got less broken over time. He still rides a bike and listens to WBAI. On weekends he volunteers at a public boathouse where he works outtake.

Nathan updated the printer FAQ to include the 8500 cartridge sensor. He is still a teacher.

Claire went back to stealing classes at Columbia. This ended after 9/11 because Columbia got new IDs with holograms.

Hook and gear were salvaged by a store in San Francisco called Scrap. The pair were sold as art supplies and became part of a whirligig that now lives in North Carolina. If there is any kind of breeze, they spin together.

ACKNOWL

EDGMENTS

1. Back up your data. It doesn't take that long.

2. Things were made up in this book, but the history of Tekserve is pretty true (tho not thorough or complete). I would like to thank David Lerner and Dick Demenus for creating Tekserve. Huge thanks to the former Tekserve employees I talked to who shared their memories and stories: PLB, DMD, JVL, AL, DY, JS, NS, DT, TJ, MW, WB, HJG, TY, VS, and PS.

3. Bless you, Xerox Phaser 6180DN, despite the "transfer life" error message you have displayed for the past two years. Thank you to my brothers and sister for letting me have all of my dad's toner after he died. Thanks to Apple for making computers that I love to an illogical degree.

4. Extra large thanks to Sean McDonald, my editor. Thanks to the FSG art department, and Anna Stein.

5. The bumper pages were inspired by the program Print Shop for the Apple II. The chapter icons are 32 pixels wide and drawn by me, for fun.

6. No, for real, go back up your data right now.

A Note About the Author

Tamara Shopsin is a renowned illustrator, graphic designer, writer, part-time cook, and co-owner of the New York City eatery Shopsin's. She is the author of *Mumbai New York Scranton*, *What Is This?*, and *Arbitrary Stupid Goal*; and coauthor, with Jason Fulford, of the books *This Equals That* and *Offline Activities*.